Mythos of the Door

Mythos of the Door

Door County, Wisconsin Poems

FOUR WINDOWS PRESS | STURGEON BAY, WISCONSIN

Thomas Davis and Four Windows Press
231 N Hudson Ave.
Sturgeon Bay, WI 54235
 www.fourwindowspress1.com

Publisher's Note: This is a work of poetry. Names, characters, and incidents are a product of the author's imagination. Locales and public names are sometimes used for poetic purposes. Any resemblance to actual people, living or dead, or to businesses, companies, events, institutions, or locales is completely coincidental.

Book Layout © 2017 BookDesignTemplates.com

Mythos of the Door. -- 1st ed.

ISBN: 978-0-9991957-5-8

Cover photo: Cave Point in Winter
by Ethel Mortenson Davis

Dedication

To my daughters, Sonja Bingen and Mary Wood, who ensured we moved to Sturgeon Bay in Door County

And, as always

To Ethel, the love of my life

Acknowledgements

"The Dragon Mages," March 2022. *Moss Piglet*, John Bloner, Jr., ed., pp. 44-45.

"Spirit Bear," "Spirit Bear," *Wisconsin Poets Calendar 2017*, Francha Barnard and Estella Lauter, eds., p. 20.

"Goose Thunder," *Wisconsin Poet's Calendar 2016*, Brenda Lempp and Carol Bishop, ed. (Eau Claire, WI: Wisconsin Fellowship of Poets, 2016).

"Country of the Bears," *Moss Piglet*, John Bloner, Jr., ed., January 2023, p. 75.

"Shades of Geese Dredged of Time," published in *Prophecy of the Wolf*. 2023. All Things That Matter Press.

"In the Aftermath," published in *Prophecy of the Wolf*. 2023. All Things That Matter Press.

"The Cougar," published in *Prophecy of the Wolf*. 2023. All Things That Matter Press.

"The Eagle and the Pelican," published in *Prophecy of the Wolf*. 2023. All Things That Matter Press.

"Woman, Wolf, and Bear," *Lothlorien Poetry Journal Blog*. Strider Marcus Jones, ed. (UK: accessed 7/27/22 at https://lothlorienpoetryjournal.blogspot.com

"The Raven's Croak," *An Ariel Anthology* (Washburn, WI: Ariel Woods Books, 2014), p. 44.

"Four Black Cormorants," *Lothlorien Poetry Journal Blog*. Strider Marcus Jones, ed. (UK: accessed 7/27/22 at https://lothlorienpoetryjournal.blogspot.com

Poems published in, *In the Unsettled Homeland of Dreams*. 2019. All Things that Matter Press:

"Inflamed Imagining," p. 3.

"Freedom's First Night, Before Dawn," p. 14.

"Like Moses in the Wilderness," p. 24.

"The Bridge That Was a Wall," p. 35.

"Miracle Inside a Storm from Hell," p. 43

"Inside the Turning of Time," p. 52.

"A Force Inside the Dream of God," p. 59.

"The Place Where Joy and Hope are Made," p. 67.

"Chicago on the Road to Freedom," p. 78.

"A Scow in a Warehouse," p. 87.

"Emerging into Freedom," p. 97.

"Arrival of a Prophet in Washington Island's Wilderness," p. 109.

"Lives Lived as Prayers," p. 119.

"Beneath the Waves, Above the Waves, a Song of Death and Light,"
     p. 127.
"The Vagaries of Time," p. 136.
"The Metamorphosis of Zeal," p. 144.
"The Transmutation of Desperation," p.151.
"Words' Consequence," p. 158.
"Religion as Whiteness," p. 167.
"Chicago's Gift," p. 175.
"Beyond Fear and Depression," p. 185.
"Throwing Off Old Chains," p. 197.
"In the Throes of Having Lost Expected Love," p. 208.
"The Work of Hope and Dreams in Being Human," p. 217.
"Washington Island Ice," p. 226.
"A Time of Aftermaths," p. 235.
"The Healing Human Spirit," p. 244.
"An Incident on Washington Island," p. 255.
"Remembering a Winter Sky," p. 265.
"From Inside the Gates of New Jerusalem," p. 275.
"Love Singing Alive the Moon," p. 285.
"Upon the Edge of Sanity and Fear," p. 294.
"In the Unsettled Homeland of Dreams," p. 303.
"Aftermath," p. 310.
"Cherry Orchard," *Door County Living*, Early Summer 2016, p. 29, Alyssa
     Skiba, ed., Arts and Literature edition.
"The Pine," *Poetry Out of Wisconsin V*, Mardi Fries and Jeri McCormick,
     ed. (Madison, WI: Wisconsin Fellowship of Poets, 1980), p. 61.
"The Coming of Christmas to Washington Island," *Peninsula Pulse*, "Arts,
     Literature and Entertainment," Vol. 21, Issue 52, December 23-31,
     pp. 8-9.
"Carver of Birds," *Lothlorien Poetry Journal Blog*. Strider Marcus Jones, ed.
     (UK: accessed 7/27/22 at https://lothlorienpoetryjournal.blog-
     spot.com/?fbclid=IwAR12U7vGs6xfgEelERQwJZ5Qf5yM7xP41n
     DRivrWJWtBt6o67j9bHC_OtGQ.
"Planting the Wings of Monarch Butterflies," *An Ariel Anthology*, edited
     by Deanna Yost (Washburn, WI: Ariel Woods Books, 2015), p. 48.
"When an Artist Drew an Owl's Portrait," "2020 Hal Prize Poetry Win-
     ners," *Peninsula Pulse*, honorable mention, October 6, 2020, accessed
     at https://doorcountypulse.com/2020-hal-prize-poetry-winners,
10/11/20.

Table of Contents

The Americans

Reflections

Introduction

My wife, Ethel Mortenson Davis, and I moved to Sturgeon Bay on the Door Peninsula after I retired as Provost of Navajo Technical University, which has campuses in both New Mexico and Arizona in the Navajo Nation. Our two daughters had decided we should move to Sturgeon Bay after my retirement so that we could be close to the two of them and our four grandchildren. At that time, we were also still grieving the untimely death of our 27-year-old son, Kevin, from cancer.

Our daughters had picked out our house on North Hudson Avenue for us since we had not had time to come house hunting before we made the move from Continental Divide in New Mexico to Wisconsin. We drove up to the house in the dark, looking for a red picket fence our picture of the house had shown, unloaded our two dogs, and then camped out until a moving van arrived the next day with beds and furniture.

Retirement at first was a major challenge. I had been the Provost, President, Acting President, and Chief Academic Officer at tribal colleges and universities in New Mexico, Nebraska, Minnesota, and Wisconsin, with one small stint developing a virtual college for Bay Mills Community College in Northern Michigan, and I was used to being incredibly busy. At Navajo Technical University there were, often, people waiting in the parking lot to catch me before I got to my office, and that kind of constant meeting with students, faculty, and others continued as I wrote grants, worked on accreditation issues, tried to inspire the faculty to develop new curriculum, and helped run the university.

Thankfully, the President of Navajo Tech, Elmer Guy, had given me enough tasks to work on so that I could spend at least a few hours a day on a mixed bag of university activities, but my new reality was unlike anything that I had experienced for decades. I wasn't pressed to work 9 to 12 hours a day, overwhelmed by trivial and crucial deadlines, and I didn't know what to do with myself. Within a month of having arrived in Door County, one of the most exciting places on earth that attracts millions of tourists during tourist season, I fell into a deep depression.

My salvation came when I reflected on the best experiences Ethel and I had during our years in New Mexico. Every Sunday, for years, we had driven a little over an hour to the Inscription Rock Trading Post in El Morro for a poetry group that came to be called the Zuni Mountain Poets.

Out of that experience I had written two books, *Inside the Blowholes* and *The Weirding Storm*, an epic poem.

I had written four previous books, *Sustaining the Forest, the People, and the Spirit*, a non-fiction essay and history on the sustainable forestry of the Menominee Indian tribe, *The Alkali Cliffs*, my first novel that I had finished during the end of my experience working with Dr. Verna Fowler to found the College of the Menominee Nation, *An American Spirit*, a formal epic poem, and a children's novel I had written for my grandson, William, called *Salt Bear*, which told an adventure tale involving salt bears, jackalopes, and a cactus buck, mythical creatures of the American west.

What was different about the writing I was doing during our years meeting with the Zuni Mountain poets was different in that those books were an exploration of the place where we were living. The books I had previously written had been primarily driven by my lifelong desire to become a published writer. *Inside the Blowholes* had a group of dragons as characters that lived in the El Malpais National Monument, a place with lava tubes and large sinkholes where giant lava flows have created an otherworldly landscape that mixes pygmy forest, pinyon, juniper, and ponderosa trees, of the high desert and the contours of the Zuni mountains with miles of strange rock formations and volcanic ash. The dragons in *The Weirding Storm*, at least in my mind, were ancestors that, deep in mythical history, explained the El Malpais dragons' existence.

Struggling with depression in our new home and reading a lot of Shakespeare, Chaucer, and old English and American poetry, I concluded that great poetry is an exploration into place, self, time, relationships, and the times in which poets live. The exploration can come from conscious or unconscious mind, result in poetry that is absolutely clear or contains a mystery requiring the reader to search for meaning, but it never ends up where it started with the first impulse to write the poem. I also woke up to a title one morning after a restless night, *Mythos of the Door*, that gave me a theme for a journey that could duplicate what had driven my creativity in New Mexico.

I forced myself to start writing poetry. The first poems were formal verse using the old forms, continued out of the experience of using iambic pentameter for *The Weirding Storm* and *An American Spirit*. I wasn't opposed to free verse. Who could ever deny the importance of Walt Whitman as a poet? I had written a lot of free verse poems. I understood traditional verse forms are not in vogue, especially not with the most important journals publishing poetry. But *The Weirding Storm* had been published by Bennison Books in Great Britain, so, publishable, or not, I committed myself to exploring the mythos of the door, place and metaphor. What other place has a deadly water passage called *Buttes des Mortes*? Death's Door?

A mythos is a myth or mythology, a traditional theme or plot structure, or a set of beliefs of assumptions. The first poems were written out of my years in Indian country while still exploring the past of the Door peninsula, but then my exploration led into history, the landscape, the people, and relationships found in both nature and humans.

I hope I have succeeded in discovering a mythos that will intrigue readers and help them to come to some understanding of a contemporary world too often in chaos. Sometimes to look forward, you need to look back, and sometimes you need to explore beneath the surface of tales and lyrics to find larger meanings that celebrate lives we all have alone and together.

There are notes I want to make before ending this. First, most, though not all, poems in this volume use iambic meter, although the rhyme scheme, when I am not writing blank verse, is varied, ranging from couplets to those found in a variety of old forms. There are seven types of sonnets, the craft of which is described at the end of the book. Not all are 14 lines long, though all are traditionally considered sonnets.

The sonnet sequence, "In the Unsettled Homeland of Dreams," was originally published in my historical novel with the same title that is about seven black families who fled the bootheel of Missouri via the Underground Railroad before the Civil War and settled on Washington Island where they established a fisher's community. I started the sequence early in my effort to explore the mythos of the Door. This was before I began to write the novel. In the novel each sonnet introduces a chapter. Putting this volume together, I wanted to explore how the group of poems holds up as a sequence.

Two poems have been added to the sequence, neither of which are sonnets. Ralph Murre occasioned at least one of those poems when he asked, after reading the novel, what happened to the Mississippi River? You cannot get from Missouri to Wisconsin without crossing the Mississippi. I answered him with the blank verse poem, "1845: Crossing the Mississippi on the Underground Railroad." The other poem is found before the sequence starts.

Most of the poems are either narrative or lyric, a requirement for a book exploring the mythos where place is one of the predominant themes. There is a touch of free verse, especially toward the end where I present three Ekphrastic poems drawn from three of Door County's plethora of galleries, a contemporary type of poetry Ethel and I tried our hand at under the tutelage of the late Francha Barnard, one of Door County's tribe of poets.

Not long after I started writing these poems, my depression went away and has stayed away. Ethel was writing her poetry and creating pastel masterpieces almost from the day we moved into our small house, and then we discovered the Dickenson Poetry Series at the United Unitarian Church in Ephraim and then the Unabridged group containing some of the best poets anywhere. Thus, what started in depression evolved into celebration, the mythos of the Door.

Thomas Davis
Sturgeon Bay, Wisconsin
12/25/2022

A further note is that I owe a grateful thank you to Ethel and Mike Orlock, both of whom read this book in its entirety and helped improve it in the process. The monthly meetings of our Unabridged Poetry Group at Write On Door County also helped me improve many of the poems.

In the Mists of Time

The Dragon Mages
In Caves Beneath Washington Island

To John Stevens (Looker) and Nick Moore

The dragon, deep inside the earth, the cave
Warmed by the bubbling natural pool,
Its scales half-moons that glistened blue
In light that emanated from the fires
That seemed refracted off a mirror's shine,
Stared at the mages' mumbling sing-song words.

Their incantations changed from spoken words
That echoed through the darkness of the cave
Into a rain of rainbows, dropping shine
Into the watered depths inside the pool.
The dragon's eyes began to whirl with fires
Intense with cold and sparks of sapphire blue.

As light shot out from dragon eyes, a blue,
Dark luminescence glowed with rainbow words
That seemed as if they burned with endless fires
As timeless as the dark inside the cave.
The mages' eyes, the dragon's eyes began to pool
A meaning from the deep, dark water's shine.

"Time is a watch," the first mage said. "A shine
That lets a human get through heartaches blue
Enough to color universes, pool
Through generations into endless words
That forms an understanding of the cave
That makes of human minds great human fires."

"Time is the earth," the young mage said. "It fires

Up summers long with sun, then brings fall shine
To forests dancing red and gold as winter's cave
Spreads fields of snow beneath skies' frigid blue
Until the birds of spring begin to sing and words
From poets makes the world a spring-fed pool."

The blue-scaled dragon blinked its swirling pool
Of rainbow eyes and flicked its tongue at fires
Beyond the sight of mages, made its words
Into a stream of images, a shine
That showed the Book of Time as water, blue,
That bubbles warmth into a deep earth cave.

And time spun from the darkness of the cave
Into the world above, and skies shined blue
As hearts lived lives inside time's endless shine.

Spirit Bear

As dark as night, as gray as slate, a bear
Rose from a foaming wave and walked to shore.
Above gray limestone cliffs a fiery glare
Of maples bent into the tempest's roar.

Out in the lake clouds churned a waterspout
Into a weave of water, waves, and sky
As frenzied schools of salmon, whitefish, trout
Leapt from the wind-whipped waves and tried to fly.

The bear, eyes black as lodestone, stood and roared
Into the roar of waves and shrieking wind
And tipped its massive head, its voice a chord
That stilled the storm and brought it to an end.

As winter gnarled inside the bear's black eyes,
Its breath spilled geese into the lake and skies.

Goose Thunder

All week green waves had groaned and cracked great chunks
Of gleaming ice onto the bay's curved shore.
Then waves of geese, wings arched, began to pour
Onto the shining lake—small, gabbling monks
Dark-cowled in heaven's shining, winding trunks
Of bodies stirred by Spring's *esprit de corps*
As gabble after gabble, more and more,
Became a mass as open waters shrunk.

A V of snow geese, flying white through wind,
Swooped down upon the lake. A darkness stirred,
A whirling vortex wild, as honking cries
Became a waterspout so large it dimmed
The lake into a shadow, waters blurred
By roiling, whirring-dark, goose-rising skies.

Snow Blowing Through an Empty Field

Albino deer emerge from banks of snow
Into the moonlight of the winter night.
The sheen of silver from the ghostly glow
Of luminance stained from the full moon's light
Spreads through the shadows where the snow's soft white
Moves with the movement of the silent deer.

The maple trees begin to stir, a slight
Breath silent through a sky pristinely clear.
A huge tree cracks. A wave of startled fear
Jerks through the deer. A wind begins
To blow through barking trees, the atmosphere
Alive with movement as the moonlight spins
Light dancing through an empty field that flows
With running waves of ghostly pure white does.

Country of the Bears

He walked into the world of bears, black eyes,
Furs brown, white, black, and even sometimes reddish,
A murmuring of growling every way
He turned or cocked his head to try to hear.
The smell was overwhelming too, a pungency
That let him know he'd left his human world.

And in the air, a substance, dream-weird, filled
With power from another, more ancient time,
Seemed like mist that hung beyond the place
His mind could perceive, wild chimera sparked
With forks of lightning trunked beneath sky
And earth, tales webbing past and future, now,
Into the arrow of time that had no end,
No starting point, a chaos beautiful
And terrifying even if it made no sense
But still contained the sense of universe.

The bears ignored him, walking into caves,
Snouts stained from berries,
Until a grizzly, eight feet tall, turned, stood
On its hind legs, looked into his eyes
And foxed into his head a full, white moon
So large it filled a crow-black, starless sky
With washing light and let him see the sun,
Reality congealed from who bears are,
Scales and skins of animals where beasts
Are human, human beasts, and earth
Is made of life full-blown in emptiness
Stretching time between great fields of stars.

"This is the land of bears," the great bear said.

And in the words, he heard the message meant,
The vision dredged from memories that echoed
Through time not really space or time,
But who we humans really are, bears are,
The earth is as we find ourselves inside
The world of snuffling, growling, talking bears.

Woman, Wolf, and Bear

As cold as morning mist upon a hill
Above the lake that danced light from the sun,
The woman stood and felt a warning chill
That screamed at her and made her want to run,
But, frozen, scared, she turned toward the wood
And shadows where a massive white wolf stood.

She did not move. The wolf's wild, pale green eyes
Stared balefully at her, its body tense
With energies she somehow felt, the skies
Above them darkening with clouds so dense
A twilight lengthened shadows, made her feel
A rush of fear she thought she should conceal.

Eyes fixed on her; the wolf stepped from the trees
So slowly that she barely saw him move.
She could not make her rigid legs unfreeze,
But stared back at the wolf as if to prove
The fear she felt was courage free of fear
Though pale green eyes, half closed, made death seem near.

The wolf crouched down as if to spring at her,
But then its head jerked north toward a stand
Of young white pine, eyes concentrated, fur
Around its neck alive. The woman's hand
Moved, broke paralysis. A great gray bear
Rose up inside the pines, the wolf's cold glare.

The bear glanced at the woman as she backed
Away from wolf and bear, then, anthracite
Inside its eyes, glared at the wolf, strength stacked
Against a spirit brimming with a light

That darkened morning skies and choked the day
With time suspended as it stalked its prey.

The great bear roared. The white wolf bared its teeth
And growled, its spirit kicking up a breeze
That blew into the bear's black eyes beneath
A dead still canopy, the forest's trees
Now covered with a brooding, bristling night
Contrasting with the wolf's bright, shining white—

And then the wolf was gone, the bear alone.
It stared at where the wolf had stood and felt
The emptiness beneath the trees, the drone
Of singing wind as rain began to pelt
The ground and run-in muddy rivulets
That clouded in the bear's stirring spirit.

At last, the bear dropped down and stuck its claws
In earth, the human woman haunting him:
The fear inside her eyes, the wolf's white paws
Prepared to spring into the stunning hymn
Of beauty circling her, the way she held her head
As wolf's eyes counted her as prey soon dead.

The bear sniffed stormy air and found the path
She'd used to flee the wolf and him and stalked
Toward impossibility, an aftermath
That could not be, that mocked him as he walked
In air perfumed with beauty's human scent,
A woman's song of being, heaven sent.

Shades of Geese Dredged Out of Time

The old man walks into the cedar forest.
Cold waves rise up to thunder white-capped rage
Against dark dolostone cloaked white with snow.
The twisted trunks of trees, born in an age
Long past, reach out into the old man's path
And clutch at bearskin boots as black as night.
Time whorls as lightning jags above the slate
Of waves, and thunder dances cloudy light
Into a rush of wilding, whistling wind.

The old man stands upon a cold, high ledge
Inside the weirding winter of the storm
And stares at ice congealed from clouds of mist
That glitter as a shining spray transforms
The frigid air into a swirl of light
Reflecting darkness from the dolostone.
The old man sighs, and in an ancient voice
Begins to sing, his voice a toneless drone.

Out of the icing mist a flock of geese
Fly wings a whir, from cresting, foaming waves.
Behind them shades of geese, dredged out of time,
Come streaming from the darkness of the caves
Beneath the old man's ledge shined black with ice.
The old man lifts his arms and tries to see,
Inside the mist of time, what fate is threaded
Into the heartbeats of humanity.

The cedar forest snakes its roots through stone.
The storm's crescendo rises as the lightning
Disperses fire above the raging waves.
Snow whips through wind, a hail-hard stinging

That bites through deerskin clothes into chilled flesh
And brings cold tears into the old man's eyes.
Tears freeze; the geese shades disappear; the man
Stands blind beneath the fury of the skies.

In the Aftermath

The woman wrapped the child against the cold
And walked into the forest where the glow
Of moonlight cast a deeply shadowed gold
Beneath the trees on softly shining snow.

She gathered wood, the baby on her back,
And built a fire, its warmth a dancing light
Upon a great flat rock protruding black
Into the lake's infinity of white.

Then, in the dark, sat, death-still, beside
The flames, the baby in her arms, the smear
Of stars above their heads a radiant tide
Of silence singing to the ebbing year.

At last, her voice a permutation slipped
Into the night, she started chanting words
Born deep in spirit as the blackened crypt
Of waters stirred beneath lake ice, and birds,

As black as mourning shrouds, began to fly,
The forest stirring like the waters, wind
A whisper as the baby voiced a tiny cry
And shadowy trees began to sway and bend.

The woman got up on her feet, her voice
As silver as the moon, and sang as deer
Began to bound onto the ice: "Rejoice,"
The woman sang, and as she sang the fear

Felt during hours of pain-filled, labored birth
Dissolved into the biting wind and light

That danced with deer upon the lake, the earth
And living integrated with the night.

The Eagle and the Pelican

The day was shining, water dancing blue
Below the hill still glittering with dew.
Achat, with Hurit by his side, looked down
Toward the pebble beach and lake, his frown
Intense with memories he'd long suppressed,
His heartbeat beating loudly in his chest.
Long years had passed since he had stood above
The place reminding him of timeless love.

His childish body hid behind a birch
Inside a grove upon the hill, his perch
The perfect place to watch his father run
Toward his mother on the beach, the sun
So bright with summer heat it bent the air
And danced above the terror of despair.

That night his father, in a shallow cave,
Had whispered, "When it's light, you'll have to save
Yourself by hiding. They won't try to kill
Your Mom and me. They want you dead. Your skill
In hiding where you can't be found is all
The hope that's left." His mother's night-bird call
Had told them she was near. "Remember, hide!"
He'd said, then left the cave, his son inside.

Five hunters left the trees. His father ran.
His mother stopped and watched. The biggest man
Stood still, pulled bow string, let an arrow fly.
It struck his father's back. His mother's cry
Of anguish shattered silence as the big man's yell
Of triumph echoed when his father fell.

A boy of ten, he knelt and watched the men
Walk slowly down the beach, knives drawn, a grin
Upon their faces as his mother cried
Until the bloody moment when she died.

As Hurit watched the shadows on his face,
Tears welled into her eyes. "This is the place?"
She asked. He stared into the distant past
And felt the shock and terror that had gasped
Into his spirit, forced him up the hill.
"Not here," he said. "Up there. I saw them kill
My mother and my father here. I fled
So that I wouldn't have to see them dead."

He turned abruptly, climbing up toward
The cliffs above them. As an eagle soared
From off the rising rocks, Achat stopped, glanced
At Hurit, beautiful and strong, entranced
By mysteries she did not understand.

He felt his twisted back and twisted hand
Send shudders through the villagers who looked
At him. His gross deformities had hooked
A terror that their spirits could not shake
No matter how his parents tried to make
Him like another boy, a villager
And not some dark, unholy, malformed cur.

The eagle circled from the cliffs to where
He climbed, its piping cries a solitaire,
Bleak ritual that seemed to integrate
Their movements with an augury of fate.

The men upon the beach had seen him climb
Into the open. Scared and grieving, time

A shrinking leather strap about his neck,
He started scaling up the cliffs, a speck
Of darkness in the sky above him, fear
Inside each breath he took, his thoughts not clear.
At last, upon the cliff rim, looking down,
He watched the hunters' point, an eagle's brown,
Swift body suddenly above the cliffs,
A pelican below the eagle, riffs
Of offshore winds a trembling under wings
That folded as a beak's bright yellow flings
Into the flying pelican as two
Large birds fall tumbling through the sky's bright blue.

As blood spewed from the pelican, dense mist
Spread from the blood, a shadowy encyst
So thick it blinded him; he lost his sight.
The summer day had turned into a night
So dark he could not move. He tried to hear
The hunters at the cliff's rock base, a queer
Infinity inside his head, but all
He heard were whispers in the murky pall
That chilled his bones and goaded him to see
Again the murderous, wild sense of glee
That plunged a knife into his mother's heart
And tore his sense of who he'd been apart.

As Hurit took his hand upon the rim
Above the cliff and bay, he looked so grim
He frightened her. "This is the place," she said.

He felt the awful sense of blinding dread
That once had paralyzed him as he stood
In mist, the hunters out of sight, childhood
A past forgotten. "When my father came
And led me from this cliff," he said. "My shame

At having hidden as my parents died
Was more than I could take. I thought the tide
Of life had ended, leaving me a husk
Who'd live his life inside an endless dusk.
I never thought I'd love or feel again.
My living felt as if it was a sin."

"My father found you in a cedar swamp,"
She said.
                "He frightened me," he said. "The clomp
Of boots through muck continued what assailed
Me while I dreamed of dying, as I railed
Against my hands and back and longed for death."

"My father said he heard your rasping breath
Before he found you on a spit of land,"
She answered. "When you couldn't even stand
He carried you. He's always said he knew
That you were someone special, someone who
Would give to all our people special gifts."

He looked down at the beach below the cliffs.
He saw the arrow in his father's back
And saw his mother as a spirit, black
Eyes urging him to run, his father's voice
An insubstantial whisper sapping choice
About continued living from his will,
His father's running swift but, yet, dead still.
A guttural howling haunted hate into his eyes.
He heard again his mother's anguished cries.

"I watched you save my mother's life," she said,
Voice soft. "You took the fever from her head
And put it in the air. I saw you call
Old Weso back from death, the awful pall

Of waxen lifelessness inside his skin,
His face all twisted by his death-mask grin."

He took a deep, long breath. The eagle flew
Above their heads. The sunlight seemed to skew
Into a twisted ball of blinding light.
The eagle disappeared, its soaring flight
An emptiness of bright blue summer sky.

Inside his head the pelican's sharp cry,
As eagle talons sank into its flesh,
Forged summer light into an augured mesh
That jolted fire into a boy that made
His way through mist behind his father's shade.

He looked at Hurit and his twisted hand.
He felt the power in the cliffs, this land.
He wondered, as he stared at distant waves,
Why he was looking at his parent's graves.

The Cougar

The cougar, tawny shadow in the rocks,
Moved stealthily toward the maple grove.
Lake water glinted as the noisy flocks
Of geese stormed from the shelter of the cove.
The blinding sunlight still allowed the moon
To sail, ghost-white, into the dying afternoon.

Far out, a dozen miles from land, the swells
Of rocking waves beneath the tiny boat,
A man begins to celebrate and yells,
Emotions unaware of how remote
He is from land, the glistening chinook
Caught by the white bone of his hand-carved hook.

The winter's done, he thought. At last, it's done!
He reached down for his paddle as a haze
Crept from the north and dimmed the western sun.
He felt a change inside the rolling waves
And saw how far he'd traveled from the trees
That shivered from a sudden, chilling breeze.

The cougar tensed its body on a ledge
Above a trail deer followed to the lake.
All day it fixed its eyes upon a hedge
The deer would file around, the bloody rake
Of claws in deer flesh promised in the way
It waited patiently throughout the day.

Clouds scudded black into the evening skies
As choppy waves began to spray the wind
Into the man's cold face and reddened eyes.
At last, his mind began to apprehend

The danger in the darkness of a night
Directionless without a hint of light.

A doe and fawn came through the hedge and stopped.
The cougar did not move. Time froze. The doe
Kept staring at the ledge. At last ears dropped.
The cougar watched the fawn, its cautious, slow,
Small movement made toward the cougar's claws
Retracted, still, inside its twitching paws.

The mother snorted at the fawn. It flinched
Toward a maple trunk. The cougar sprang,
Its body twisting in the air, jaws clinched
As doe and fawn leapt through an overhang
Of cedars as the cougar hit the ground
And filled the silent woods with snarling sound.

Inside the rhythm of his paddling
The man began to dream of children's eyes.
Outside the wind was constant, rattling
The thick bark walls he'd built, the haunting cries
Of winter deprivation in the breath
Of little ones too young to face their death.

Hours passed. He fought the waves. The shore
Somewhere inside the darkness beckoned him.
He dug into his tiredness, past the core
Of whom he was, his perseverance grim
Enough to face the dance of spirits howled
Across awareness where disaster prowled.

Then, suddenly, the boat hit land. It threw
Him backwards. Lying still he felt life surge
Its song into his beating heart, the brew
Of wind and waves no longer like a dirge

Of doom, the willow basket full of fish—
Fulfillment of his family's anxious wish.

The cougar's eyes were fire. The man had placed
The basket on the pebble beach and pulled
The boat above the water when he faced
The cat, its eyes and crouching body bold
Beside the basket with the fish, it's ears
Laid back, it's growling stirring ancient fears

Of children, grieving with their mother, left
Alone inside a wilderness, the man's
Life gone, their futures suddenly bereft
Of all the dreams he'd fashioned from his plans.
The cougar's eyes were suns, a universe.
The man waved arms and shouted out a curse.

The cougar turned and grabbed a fish, the night
A darkness swallowing a shadow bled
Into an emptiness devoid of light.
The man stood frozen as the cougar fled.
At last, he got the basket, climbed the hill,
The cougar in his life-force, tense and still.

The Yellow Eyes

1

The whiteness wailed with wind-swept waves of snow.
Upon the ice, a dozen miles from land,
The huge man walked into the vertigo
Of emptiness and bitter cold that spanned
Horizons darkening into a night
Intense with clouds that suffocated light.

He heard the wolf before he saw its eyes
Gleamed yellow in accumulating dark.
Its panting separated from the cries
Inside the wind so subtly that the spark
Of fear that nearly made his legs give way
Seemed like the rhythm of the dying day.

The great wolf, coat as black as anthracite,
Loomed like a shadow from a stinging wave
Of snow, a darkness darker than the night,
A vision dredged from dreams born in a grave.
A heavy tiredness weighed inside the man.
The wolf kept eyes upon the path he ran.

As hours passed hours the universe became
A movement shared between the man and wolf.
The storm died down. At dawn a yellow flame
Along the far horizon's edge unveiled a roof
Of clouds that felt as if they were a vice
Pressed down upon the endless miles of ice.

The man kept staring at the white expanse
Stretched endlessly away from where they were.

He felt his spirit caught inside a trance
Transforming time into a senseless blur
Of wolf breath, gusts of wind, and running feet
Staccatoed, pulsing through his heart's strained beat.

As evening gathered up the winter skies,
The great wolf growled and shocked the man aware.
The yellow eyes looked deep into his eyes.
The storm swirled deep inside the untamed stare.
He stopped. The wolf stopped, growled so low
The storm stirred winds and stinging waves of snow—

And then the wolf was gone into the trees
That forested the hills above the rocky shore.
Alone, but near to land, still not at ease,
He walked toward the cedars bent before
Him like a haven from the plains of white
As suddenly the ice was bathed in light.

2

Years later, sitting by a council fire
As dancers danced the heartbeat of the drum,
A wailing howl rose from the forest, dire
As if the ending of the world had come.
The big man stood, the council's patriarch,
And walked, without a word, into the dark.

In the Time
of Changing

The Voyageurs

They hulked along the rocky shore,
Backs humped with bundled beaver hides,
Tough, bearded men whose spirits bore
The rise and fall of waves and tides

That they had ridden from the towns
Where men wore hats and women furs
And steepled churches belled sweet sounds
That blessed the treks of voyageurs.

Inside the woods a warrior stood
And watched the white men's straggly line.
He wondered how they'd seized the good
In life and stripped it of its shine.

The Potawatomi had fused
Their lives into the wilderness,
But now the whites had come, confused
The people with their willfulness

And left a forest beaver pond
Bereft of beaver, wasting life
And taking what was left beyond
The forest severed by a knife

That cut into the people's hearts
And stirred up dreams of endless wealth
As people saw how ancient truth departs,
Seized, snatched without a need for stealth.

He stood and watched the white men move
Toward the trading post they'd made.

He knew no warrior that would disapprove
What they had gotten from their trade

Of beaver pelts for goods or guns
The whites described as civilized.
He knew the tribal daughters, sons
Would pass beyond the world he prized.

He watched the white men hulk along
The rocky shore and shoulder time
Into a wind that was a song
That sounded good—but was a crime.

Past the Earth of Graves

Eyes scudded dark, a roiling rage of storm,
The poet stands upon gray rock, the roar
Of boiling waves the cruciform
Of time, the slates of history a lore
Long lost, but still inside the chanting names
That sings a weaving with the waves.

The poet waves his arms. His presence claims
The past. He reaches past the earth of graves
And strains to bring the fire of poetry
From campfires blazing in forgotten nights
Beside the ferment of a Celtic Sea
Onto a wild Wisconsin shore, old rites
Engendering a music mad with winds
That spill through words, a storm that never ends.

The Raven's Croak

Hunched down beside a woodpile, ebony,
In shadows from the cedars overhead,
The raven blinked black eyes, its dishabille
Of feathers rustling, stirring up a dread
So dark it seemed as if it called up from the dead
White wisps of spirits buried in the snow.
The raven hopped on top the woodpile, head
Cocked, moving like a dancer in a show,
A shadows' shadow pantomiming woe.

Dawn's darkness deepened as the raven leaped
Into the sky and hovered as the glow
Of blood-light saturated earth and seeped
Into the raven's eyes, its dance undone
Until its beak croaked out the blazing sun.

Four Black Cormorants

Four cormorants, crow-black, fly low above
The lake's ice, white with tints of apple green.
Upon a red roof, ravens, croaking of
The way the blue-black of their feather's sheen
Swifts shadows on the snow's white shining, preen
Into a circle, stirring whispering winds
That cause white wisps to pirouette, careen
Across the fields as daylight slowly ends.
A black cat tops a hill and then descends
Into a field where thirteen cats have made
A ring beneath a full moon; each pretends
The others aren't as eyes glow green as jade—

The wind blows cold; the snow-white moon is bright
As cormorants fly in the spell-bound night.

Lighthouse on *Buttes des Mortes* Island[1]

On moonlit nights it's like a haunted dream.
You walk alone on green, moss-covered rock
And listen to the breakers as they swish and steam
Across breakwaters as a lonely hawk,
Above the isolation, soars dark in a sky
Awash with argent from the moon's soft light
That spreads until the ambient lullaby
Of sound and light makes magic of the night.

And then, in Buttes des Mortes, a ship's full sails
Are billowed out beneath the shining moon;
The lighthouse flashes as its beamed light trails
The ship's white wake, a flowing water rune
That hints of fog, ferocious winds, and cold,
Grim tales that won't, this glowing night, be told.

---

[1] In the 1800s what is now known as Pilot Island was known as Buttes des Mortes Island after the deadly passage between Washington Island and the Door Peninsula. This sonnet was inspired by the words of Ben Fagg, a Sturgeon Bay printer, who visited the lighthouse in September of 1890.

Storm In Death's Door

Running before the wild wailing of wind,
The ship is awash with the sounds of the waves,
The cries of the sailors as they work to extend
The life of a ship that is threatened by graves
Below the dark passage the French call the Door
Out of the tumult of life, the thunder's loud roar.

Hours pass and the hull is slammed, hammered by storm.
Waves toss the ship up and then down to deep flumes.
Clouds rage in the sky as, exhausted, the sailors all swarm
To keep the sails' angles aligned so the booms
Keep pointing the prow's head into the perilous wind
As the long day keeps on scrawling, a hell with no end.

A water tornado spins down from the sky.
The thunder crescendos, a shrieking barrage
Of death song, of lightning, a banshee's cold cry.
Convulsing, the ship seems more a mirage
Than a refuge for sailors who pray to be saved
From a world that's turned wilding and wickedly depraved.

But then, with a magic that somehow seems real,
The ferment of winds and the violent sky's gale
Begins to grow calm as the sailors anneal
Stunned spirits beginning to feel the long tale
Of a ship that seemed doomed that was able to reach
A night when bright moonlight shined alive a dark beach.

Cherry Orchard

They crawled out from their canvas tent and stared
At stumps still littered through the opening
Their two-man saw had cut into the spring-
Deep twilight made by woods so thick they dared
An axe to fell a wilderness that flared
Across so many miles no bird could wing
Its way to planted orchards blossoming
Into the dream the couple, logging, shared.

So tired she barely kept her head upright,
The woman started up the morning fire.
She sighed to see the stumps that made the field
Look strange inside the early morning light,
An emptiness surrounded by the choir
Of birds in trees where she in silence kneeled.

"The canopy is peeled
Away enough to let us plant the trees,"
He said. "Their blossoms will attract the bees."

She looked and tried to tease
The cherry trees he saw into her mind,
But all she saw were stumps, work's endless grind.

Tom Bennett

He sat upon the deck and watched the island
Grow larger as they sailed toward the harbor,
A small depression down from where steep hills
Rose up into what looked to be a plateau.
They'd sailed for days and seen two British ships
Too far away to chase, but kept their eyes
Upon horizons running white capped waves
Into infinity of waters far from shores.

Tom Bennett wasn't happy where he was.
The Quakers that had rescued him the day
His master got so drunk he'd threatened him
With beatings that would end his "god-damned" life
Had been against enrollment in the Navy.

"God doesn't give men leave to fight in wars,"
His rescuer, Bill Friends, had said. "The British
Should leave America alone—but still, to fight?"
His pale blue eyes had narrowed as he'd frowned.

But freed slaves had to eat the same as others,
And when Commander Perry started searching
For blacks and poorer whites to man his ships,
He'd gone and signed the papers that had made
Him sweat through days so tense he'd grown to hate
The moment that he'd told Bill Friends he'd signed
His life into the dark holds of a ship
That Perry cursed into a fledgling navy.

He'd learned to tolerate the sound of cannons
Exploding cannon balls into the lake
As men prepared to fight a naval battle

Where only some of them would keep their lives.
He'd even learned to keep resentment buried
When men the Commodore called trash
Belittled him and other "boys" that worked
Beside their whiteness through long, endless days.

"Rock Island," Workhorse Balin said behind
Where Tom kept staring at the trees that lined
The edges of the rocky cliffs and hill.
"That's what the sailors say that island's called.
They're saying fishing here is paradise."

Tom didn't answer. What was there to say?
And then he heard a Bible verse inside his head

> *And I saw a new heaven and a new earth:*
> *for the first heaven and the first earth were passed away;*
> *and there was no more sea.[2]*

He didn't see the battle of Put-In-Bay
To come, the sinking of the Lawrence, the cries
Of terror as the great ship shuddered, burned,
And Perry fled and fought and turned his fortunes
Upon Niagara's decks to victory
Snatched from defeat, the turning of the war.
He didn't see the years he'd spend as words
Spun from his spirit as he dreamed up schemes
To free chained families from slavery.
He didn't see the days of freedom sought
Across free states, slave states, the underground
Where, as a preacher, he became a man.

"The Potawatomi once dominated

---

[2] Holy Bible, Revelation 21:1.

These islands," Workhorse Balin said.
"They're now an empty, waiting wilderness."

Tom Bennett waited as the ship dropped down
Its anchor, fixed into the harbor's peace.
He watched an osprey circle in the heavens,
Then hurtle down toward the water, claws
Outstretched to seize a fish that shimmered
As wings beat back into the bright blue sky.

I'll come back here, he thought. To paradise.

In the Unsettled Homeland of Dreams

A Sonnet Sequence

Inflamed Imagining: Freedom

Inside the swamp, beside a cypress tree—
White herons in the water, bullfrog croaks
A symphony as dusk, as stealthily
As cat's feet creeping up on birds, evokes
The coming night—the Preacher slowly stokes
The fire blazed in his heart and starts to sing
Songs powerful enough to loosen yokes
White masters forged through endless menacing.

The words he'd use burned deep; he felt their sting
And saw his spirit fire alive in eyes
Awake to dreams, inflamed imagining
Of days spent free beneath glad years of skies.

The darkness deepened underneath the tree.
He'd preach, he thought, then, later on, they'd flee.

Freedom's First Night, Before Dawn

The white man, with his wide brimmed hat and face
Stunned pale inside a night that breathed with sounds
From woods they'd passed through in their frantic race
Against the coming dawn, turned back around
To look toward the barn that loomed ahead
Of where six families hid in scratchy brush.
He sighed as if he couldn't flee the dread
He felt in dark before dawn's first red blush.

"I made a space to hide you runaways,"
He said. He turned again and looked at eyes
That looked at him, cold fear a noxious glaze
Infecting even how the dreaded sun would rise.

"Six families can't escape at once," he said.
"I've got my family too. They're still in bed."

The Preacher looked into the man.
His eyes looked past white outer flesh
Into the place his soul began.
The white man turned again, the mesh

Of eyes surrounding him afraid
To move, to dream, to think they'd leave
This place before their master flayed
Their essence, made their spirits grieve.

Like Moses in the Wilderness

Like Moses fleeing from the Pharaoh's wrath
Before the miracle of waters parting,
The Preacher blazed a trail on freedom's path
As fear possessed their endless fleeing.

What was that man or woman really seeing
That passed them while they tried to run and hide?
What accident of fate would send them running
When slavers found them tired and terrified?

The Preacher prayed away grim miles and tried
To make their spirits testify that dreams
Are greater than the fear that crucified
Their faith that they could get across the streams
And past the towns that blocked their way and threatened
To let the slavers pounce and leave them bludgeoned.

The Bridge that was a Wall

The bridge, inside the night, was like a wall,
Small, wooden, unassuming, houses dark
Beside a path that seemed to be a call
To all who needed passage to embark
Upon a journey to the river's other side.
They hid in brush, mouths dry, dread strong enough
To make them sick, and, silently, wide-eyed,
Saw spectres armed with whips and iron cuffs
Stand shining where they'd have to cross the bridge
Without disturbing dogs or waking up
The people in the houses as the ridge
Beyond the river beckoned past the interrupt
That stood between their anxious dreams and where
Their breaths would breathe God's freedom from the air.

The Miracle Inside a Storm from Hell

Their misery growing as they splashed through streams
And felt huge clouds above the battered trees
That flung down branches as the sorceries
Of wind and hunger screams and screams and screams
Into their fears, their hatred, useless dreams
The Preacher cultivated with an ease
That wasn't true, not when the miseries
Of hell danced in the storm's wild, fierce extremes.

And then, as if inside a miracle,
They reached a lonely church, the raging storm
So fierce they quailed inside its crucible,
And knew the light of God, their spirits warm,
The dreams the Preacher preached so lyrical
It made them feel, inside their hell, reborn.

1845: Crossing the Mississippi on the Underground Railroad

They came upon the Mississippi late:
a moonless night, the crickets chirping loud
enough above the sound of wagon wheels
to penetrate the silence that they kept
beneath the canvas with the wagon boards
pressed hard beneath their bodies, weariness
so heavy from anxiety it seemed
as if escaping couldn't ever end.

Sam Braxton, on the wagon's seat, his voice so soft
they had to strain to hear, said, "Hold on now.
Don't move. Our father's got his big horse ferry[3].
We'll get across, and then we'll take a rest."

The wagon moved. The crickets chirped. Immense,
the universe seemed liquid, as the wheels
left land and slid onto the ferry's deck.
"Hold on," Sam Braxton said. "Hold quiet. Still."

Below the barge escaping slaves held
their breaths and felt the barge leave land behind.
They weren't sure what was happening outside
their dark, their bodies pressed into the boards.

The river Jordan, Joshua thought to himself.
He'd heard his mother talk of miracle
when God declared a man His son, a voice

---

[3] A horse ferry was a barge powered by a horse (or horses) on a treadmill.

from heaven, powerful: "With thee I am well pleased."

But then his thought was swallowed as the barge
began to move through unseen water-dark,
the gnawing worry that was all he'd known
for days denying that the river was
another stage they'd pass on freedom's trail.

They crossed the Mississippi late at night
and heard the white men move around and talk,
but stayed in darkness underneath a tarp
and didn't see the water, stars, or moon.

Inside the Turning Wheels of Time

Inside the rhythm of the wagon's wheels,
The Preacher, with his people crammed beside
Him underneath a false floorboard, untied
His consciousness from who he was, ordeals
He'd face for years now in the past, and reels
Of rainbow light exploded, amplified
A vision where he felt Ezekiel's tide
Of prophecies burn like a fire that heals.

He saw his Promised Land, boats filled with fish,
A land of gardens lush as men could wish,

And in the garden of his vision, black
As midnight skies, a shining Adam spoke
A chant so sibilant with grace the almanac
Of hours turned like the wagon wheel's spokes.

A Force Inside the Dream of God

Their stomachs ached, they felt ice cold, their eyes
Sank back into their sockets. Still, worn out,
They kept on moving, moving. When the skies
Were dark enough, they got up, brushed the flies,
Mosquitos off, shoved fear and gnawing doubt
Into their belly's' emptiness, and ran, their route
Through hills and fields, past roads, an exercise
In dreams that live on while the body dies.

But as they moved, the Preacher was a force
Inside the dream of God, a man possessed.
He would not fade. His tongue, without remorse,
Whipped legs too tired to move to movement, stressed
Them all until a blessed miracle
Made life and dreams again seem possible.

The Place where Joy and Hope is Made

Inside the barn the memories of war
As horses ate their hay and cows were fed:

Inside three men, one white, two black, the roar
Of cannon, sight and sound of men that bled
Their lives out as the living and the dead
Were showered with hot, splintering fusillades
Flung in the wave-tossed night from hell, the dread
Of battle dancing at the barricades
Of what you were in being human fades
Into the chaos burning through the night.

The Preacher frowned: "Destruction serenades
Our hearts against our spirit's holy light,"
He said. The others nodded. Each had prayed
To find the place where joy and hope was made.

Chicago on the Road to Freedom

Cacophony, noise, horses, people, smells,
A raging restlessness and energy
Unbounded from the places spirit dwells,
Infected them and made them want to flee
Their fleeing even as Chicago seethed
And made them wonder if their slavery
Was more than whips and white men wreathed
In arrogance, but something in their souls,
Their consciousness, the very air they breathed
That filled their lives with loss and empty holes
Where dreams should live and let life soar in skies
Removed from fear and all the deadly shoals
That, hidden, suddenly materialize
And snatch away a slave's most longed-for prize.

A Scow in a Warehouse

Eyes ate the boat, the scow, magnificence
Inside the run-down warehouse, shadows deep
As hours they'd spent caught in the turbulence
Of fear and hope as hours dragged by, the creep
Of wagon wheels hypnotic, straining nerves
Until the universe was dissonance,
a time and place where senses slowly swerved
toward disaster, dreaded slavery.

And then the scow, a tale the heart deserves,
A rush across huge waters as the tree
Of freedom looms upon a shore that sings
Into the longed-for land of jubilee,
A dream escaped from all the reckonings
That hovered in their souls' rememberings.

Emerging Into Freedom

Waves rolled with curving lines into the shore.
Lake Michigan horizoned into sky.
They watched a dark brown, white crowned osprey soar
Above the waves and heard its hunting cry.

Inside pinched spirits chained by slavery
And endless hours of suffocating fear,
Bonds loosened as the dream and fantasy
Of freedom suddenly seemed real, so near
To where they stood above the giant lake
They were not sure they had not reached a future
Aware of who they were, the earth awake
To spirits that had passed through deadly danger.

Inside the distant swamp they'd been but slaves.
They stood upon a hill and listened to the waves.

Arrival of a Prophet
in Washington Island's Wilderness

In the 1850s a small community of black families led by a black preacher, Bennett, settled in Washington Island's wilderness far from the slave holding states.

The old black man, eyes bright as noonday sun,
Splashed from the wooden boat onto the shore.
He lifted up his voice, the waves Death's Door
Whipped white behind him, praised the blessed Son
Of God and New Jerusalem and spun
Around, his arms held high, a troubadour
Of his escape from slavery and war
To wilderness, the role of sacristan
To fisherman and men and women freed
From whips and masters and the slaver's creed
Of dominance designed to pinch the soul
And void the human spirit's vital flame.

"Praise God!" the prophet said, the roll
Of waves against his feet. "Praise God's sweet name!"

Lives Lived as Prayers

They built outhouses first, then cleared a plot
Of pine and brush to plant their garden seed.
Out in the lake they fished, felt fear recede.

A Stockbridge Indian, while they'd hid, had brought
Them boats the night the lightning's fierce onslaught
Had blued night skies, and in the cold their need
To keep on running, hiding, mutinied
Against their strength, the freedom they had sought—

But now, around the campfire as their sense
Of freedom slowly leached away despair,
The Preacher dreamed alive the consequence
Of living on an island where the air
Loosed manumission's grace, and, as, intense,
His words rang out, their lives became a prayer.

Beneath the Waves, Above the Waves, A Song of Death and Light

Beneath Death's Door where water's rise and fall
In symphonies of restlessness and waves,
Dark ship hulks rest, Niagara, Nichols, all
Those torn apart by storms to fashion graves
Below deep currents powerful enough
To channel winds into a crucifix
That makes strong, hardened sailors want seraphs
To come and save them from the River Styx.

And then a young man in a wooden scow
Puts out a fishing line and feels a trout
Begin to thrash and pull him to the prow
Where waves spit mist and shine his shout
Of pure exuberance into the light
That dances wild into a big trout's fight.

The Vagaries of Time

The Christian fires burned deep in freedom's roots.
They settled in the island's wilderness
And let the Preacher's words become the shoots
Of hope that flourished as their fear and stress
Were relegated to the nightmare past,
The arrogance of whips and masters less
A worry than the way their lines were cast
Into the waters of the lake, the dream
Of lives unfettered suddenly a vast
Reality that strengthened self-esteem.

But then a man materialized from trees.
The past returned and, like a raging stream,
It dredged up terrifying memories
That made them feel time's shifting vagaries.

The Metamorphosis of Zeal

Waves, choppy from the wind, flashed glints of light.
The Preacher burned with words that rose from depths
Not seen by eyes and wove their meanings tight
Into the island's contours, in the steps
Of men and women trying to become
The people that they really were, souls meant
To live community, not martyrdom
To greed and power's joy in punishment.

Out on the lake the fishermen dropped lines
Into the depths, the light of who they'd be
Embodied in huge trout, bright rainbow shines
A metamorphosis of memory
Into a dream made manifest and real
By perseverance, words, the Preacher's zeal.

The Transmutation of Desperation

As God's house rose, their desperation built
Into stripped logs and fireplace stones, they felt
Cold brutalizing all their hopes, the quilt
Of winter storms a hazard as they dealt
With summer heat that generated sweat
And drained what strength was left to them from days
Of hiding, running, flinching at the threat
That gnawed at nerves and webbed them in its maze.

But then, inside four walls, the Preacher's voice
A clarion of prophecy and dreams,
Their desperation, rising from the choice
To run for freedom, seeped into the seams
Of God's house, propagating alchemy,
Transmuting fear into community.

Words' Consequence

Words ought to be just words, but when they burn
From eyes engendered by a seething soul,
Words take on flesh, create a bulging churn
That moves alive into a spreading scroll
Of years connected to the lives that roll
Into the turbulence of all humanity.

Upon a dock a white man's cold control
Of whom he is flare out his bastardly
Crazed prejudice into audacity
That stands inside his threats and hunts to find
The pathways used to flee the memory
Of chains that once bound flesh and made them blind
To hope that makes a human *human*, fashions
The consequences born of mortal passions.

Religion as Whiteness

They fought religion as a whiteness, probed
To find a way inside their lives to let
The genius centered in His love—light robed
With justice—free slaves from the numbing threat
Dredged from the God of thunder that had touched
The white race with superiority and rights
And forged the chains that bound free spirits clutched
With anguish felt through years of days and nights.

The abolitionists reached out and tried
To build invisible, faint trails the God
Of whiteness couldn't find since He denied
The wrongs done in His name and lived a fraud
That failed to comprehend how souls of men
Could see His Christianity as sin.

Chicago's Gift

The wilderness was difficult enough.
As winter loomed, they didn't have the clothes
To deal with minus zero days so tough
The winds would howl in blizzards wild with snows.

They worked, preparing, trying to avoid
The looming threat as flocks of geese and crows
Spoke prophesies about their dreams destroyed
By consequences flowing from the time
They'd spent in fleeing north, their hearts all buoyed
By freedom's lure, the promise of a paradigm
Embedded in the Preacher's fire, their trust
In New Jerusalem, deliverance the rhyme
That resonated through a paddle's thrust
Toward salvation, springtime's Eucharist.

Beyond Fear and Depression

Doubt, fear, a question asked at night, the stakes
So high they eat at confidence and sap
The energy from fire in eyes that hurled mistakes
Into the wind and laughed at how the gaps
Between success and failure complicates
The desperation drummed into the feet
Of children, men, and women daring fates
Defining who they'd been, their lives' heartbeat—

And then the Preacher sat alone and tried to grasp
How prophecies could be ambiguous
When hatred came to suddenly enclasp
The shores that terminated exodus—

But spirit born of fire transcends despair
And pulls determination from the air.

Throwing Off Old Chains

When words upon a page connect to where
Electric currents spark alive the mind,
Atrophied thoughts once bound by self, confined
Inside awareness looking, feeling, breathing air,
Begin to learn, to walk the thoroughfare
Of human revelation, knowledge, mind
From lives of those we've never known, that shined
Their possibilities into the flare
Of what a human can become or make.

The Preacher, as the Bible's verses swirled
Out from his eyes and heart, used words to snare
Free students into words designed to shake
Alive their learning in an unsafe world.

In the Throes of Having Lost Expected Love

The nightmare slipped into his sleep, the lash
Slow-moving, curled, until its black tip snapped
Into his flesh, blood oozing where it wrapped
Around his side, the welt an ugly slash
Of fire and slicing pain that made him thrash
Against the ropes that bound him, spirit trapped
Inside a silent, burning rage that mapped
Itself into his breath and made him smash
Against the white man's wall of slavery
And long for wings so strong he could fly free.

He woke, a free man who had reached his freedom,
But in the darkness as he contemplated
How life could lurch into a yawing chasm,
He mourned his true love lost, felt empty, scalded.

The Working of Hope and Dreams
In Being Human

Shape shifting swarms of gnats, their worries gnawed
At them as long days drained their energy
And taxed their strength as dreams of being free
Materialized in walls, fish caught, the songs to God
That echoed through the trees, the paths they trod
To carve from wilderness community,
A feeling of impregnability
Against gnats buzzing that in hope was fraud.

Their labors sang a hymn of glory rooted
In faith that they could toss away the past
And seize a future drenched in human sweat
As safety wrapped well-being sewn and quilted
Into days shining, stormy, overcast
With liberated time freed from regret.

Washington Island Ice

They did not notice when the mist began
To tendril off the ice, the brutal cold
Horizoned by the lake's huge winter span
Of white that wrapped them in an endless fold
That barely separated how the heavens
Knelt down with heavy clouds and fiercely gripped
Their spirits in a subtle separation
Of white from white, lake, sky an arching crypt.

Then, in a moment, rising mist became
A covering that muted any hint of sound
And made a silence suffocating flames
Of who they were, the dense, white wraparound
A spell that snuffed away direction—fog
A blinding, silent, disconcerting bog.

A Time of Aftermaths

Events can shock through lives and rip apart
The weave of hours infusing sapience
Throughout the complex expectations chart
Into the early morning radiance
Of rising sun, the comfort of continuance
Across the ceaseless ebb and flow of thought
Concealed until its conscious utterance
Shakes spirit out of heart, a juggernaut
Of self-adjusting to emotions caught
By staggering realities, the song
That is, though we have always looked for, sought
A future feeling right and good, not wrong.

But when events upset the flow of days,
What destinies are born out of malaise?

The Healing Human Spirit

Inside great pain a melancholy rises,
A sadness paring down the blood-song
Rived from normality and all the choices
That constitute our sense of right and wrong
And help us navigate the waves along
The axis of glad days without the sorrow
That surges into storms where demons throng
In feelings deadening our life's ebb-flow.

Then, from her pain, a mother feels the floe
Of ice inside her heart begin to thaw,
And though the pain burns deep, she starts to sow
A rightness that can ease the endless gnaw
Inside her heart and let a wedding's light
Leach darkness from depression's heavy night.

Incident on Washington Island

As Ambrose Betts gulped down the whiskey shot
That Gullickson had given him, his face
Was flushed, the muscles in his neck a knot
So tight he winced, his outrage out of place
Inside the cabin's half lit single room.

"A Winnebago brave! I tell you Gullickson,"
He said. "As large as life inside the gloom
Of Miner's kitchen, Bullock looking drawn,
As if he'd seen a ghost, as black as coal.
I've never seen the like before!" he yelled.
"An Indian, white man, black man like a shoal
Of pebbles on a beach. The Indian held
His hand up, said, I swear, to Bullock, 'You,'
He said. 'The first white man I ever knew.'

"Old Bullock, black as night,
Smiled with those teeth of his
So dazzlingly bright white
My head began to fizz.

"And Miner looked like God
About to haul back, smack
The Indian into sod.
A white man that is black!"

Remembering A Winter Sky

The rising sun on ice exploded fire
Upon the surface of the lake as light
Burned in the clouds, the bowl of sky a choir
Of gold and reds upon, above the white
Expanse that glinted, danced in flowing swells
That turned the universe into a trance
So stunning winter fishermen felt spells
Ensnaring them into the light's romance.

But even as the sky transfigured how
They felt their lives, the grind imbedded deep
In human hands and minds began to plow
Into the wonder that was theirs, the sweep
Of fire from other people's greed a cloud
So dark it seemed to be a burial shroud.

From Inside the Gates of New Jerusalem

And then a breeze, as gentle as a kiss,
Came billowing into the scow's white sail
Until the lake and island left travail
To sink into the water's dark abyss
Where no soul had to dream or reminisce
About days when raw courage couldn't fail
If voices were to someday tell the tale
Of how they'd found their sanctuary's bliss.

They reveled in the way the breeze confirmed
Their sense that they had found auspicious winds,
A shore where lives could live in Christendom
And flourish on a distant island bermed
With rock and soil against the storms life sends
To batter down the gates of New Jerusalem.

Love Singing Alive the Moon

Upon a shore where sheets of ice had stacked
Into a shadowed sky, the full moon round
And silver in a field of stars that tracked
The darkness with eternity, the sound
Of waves beyond the ice a lullaby
That serenaded who they were, they walked
And held each other's hands and felt the sigh
Of what they'd lived inside the talk they'd talked.

And in between their words, love sang the moon
Alive to whom their dreams said they would be
As passion beat against soft silver strewn
As light across ice shards, a filigree
That echoed pulsing waves, blood stirred, inflamed
Into two lifetimes that was love exclaimed.

Upon the Edge of Sanity and Fear

The edge where sanity and fear collide
Whirls passions that are uncontrollable
Into events that spark effects that tide
Across the barriers of shores and scull
Destruction, pestilence, a flood of woe
Fermented in assumptions drawn from trials
That litter through all human lives and flow
Like water over hopes, beliefs, denials,

And on the edge, in ferment's shifting shape,
Decisions ratchet back and forth; dreams lure
The spirit as dire consequences scrape
Against the future suddenly obscure
Enough to paralyze the strength from hands
That long to civilize life's hinterlands.

In the Unsettled Homeland of Dreams[4]

The Preacher sat upon a rocky hill
Above a cave where waters from the lake
Crashed angrily above the soaring shrill
Of gulls excited by a splashing wake
Of fish caught by the afternoon's harsh light
Flashed back into the early Fall-blue sky.

He sat upon the hill, his second sight
Unmoored and wild, and listened as the lie
He'd told himself when struggling to find
The island where his people could be free
Wrapped round reality, the awful bind
Of white men, dark men in the company
Of humankind, their kind, the hunger spun
From dreams once dreamed beneath a noonday sun.

---

[4] The title is a paraphrase from a poem by Pablo Neruda

The Abandonment of Washington Island
By the Island's Black Community

Gone. Like the waves grasshoppers make
Before a boy who runs into a field of weeds,
The news raced through the island as the seeds
Of mystery began to reawake
The sense that something sinister, a snake,
Was in the emptiness that almost pleads
To hear the shouts of children, men whose deeds
Had made their days of freedom by the lake.

Where did they go? Why did they have to flee?
The island people said, "It is a mystery."

When Craw's barn burned, the chill was palpable,
And now the black community is gone.
The news was like a fire, insatiable.
They took their fishing boats and fled at dawn.

*The mystery of the disappearance of seven black families, presumably run-away
slaves, from Washington Island in the 1850s persists today.*

The Americans

The Pine

"Well," Paul was saying, "I'd as soon leave the pine.
That way I'd know the thing and have it out
Where everyone could see the what of what
And not be wondering about the truth
And whether it was just a tale or dream.
If eyes can see, then brains can know."

"Well, I don't know," Pike said. "That tree's so tall. . ."

"The country's big!" Paul said. "Tall trees are tall.
But still, I've never seen the like of this!
What will they say a hundred years from now?
Especially if it's written down and made
Into some type of news that's history past.
'Why, what?' they'll say. 'A tree so tall that skies
And moon and stars and sun and even wind
Were forced to go around its soaring tall?
Come on! We future fools are not the fools
That built our future up on tales and dreams.
We used good mortar, bricks, and long, hard thought.
You'll not put anything of fancy here.
We know the ways of nature and of man,
And neither one's so tall."

         "Perhaps," Pike said.
"But then the country's not so big that trees
Can stand in way of lumber. Let's bring it down.
No one can hear us but the wind and sky,
And even they don't care for trees so tall.
One day a jagged branch will catch the sun
And tear a hole of night into its side.

We'll seal our lips and send it cut in boards.
No one will write it down. No one will know."

Then, with a shrug and nod, they cut it down.

The Exotic Birds

They spilled out of the boat like birds,
The women colorful
With parasols and dresses bright
As rainbows wonderful

Beneath a shining summer sky,
The men in suits and hats
So formal that you would have thought
They all were diplomats.

The loggers that had driven down
Onto the dock with logs
Intended for Chicago's piers
Sneered at the dandys' togs.

They laughed to see such city folk
Debark into a place
So rude the streets were packed down dirt
And spittoons were high grace.

"We'll take a wagon to the cave,"
A woman brightly said.
"A perfect picnic day!" exclaimed
A man whose face flushed red.

One logger pulled his beard and looked
Bemused to see the souls
He'd spent a year with as they mocked
Exotic birds like ghouls.

"A man could build a boarding house
And do all right, I bet,"

He said. "There's money in those clothes.
The wealthy picnic set!"

An ancient who had been around
The dock for years and years
Scoffed at this fancy, shook his head,
And waggled both his ears.

"This is an untamed wilderness,"
He barked. "Nobody serves
A plate of tea and biscuits in this place.
There's beer, not peach preserves

Baked cute by dainty looking maids
For women dressed as if
The world was civilized and neat
And not a wild-eyed stiff!"

He laughed as peacocks strutted past
Oblivious to words
That couldn't ruin a picnic day
For tourists dressed like birds.

The Sinking of the Erie L. Hinkley, October 3rd, 1903

The passengers were tired, the evening's skies
A little dark, but not that dark.
Across the bay, Egg Harbor was the place
They'd leave the Hinkley, eat a meal,
Then find their boarding house and sleep.

The squall came up so suddenly
The steamship's sailors didn't see
The green-black ugliness that swirled
Into the waves and raged the wind
And rain into a whipping wall that swept
Across the deck and staggered those
Who'd missed the strangeness in the sky.

"It's quite a squall," the captain said.

And then a monster wave rose up
And slammed into the wooden hull.
The ship began to groan as bricks
Down in the cargo hold were thrown
Against the hull and water poured
Into the space below the decks.

Upside, waves swept the passengers
And crew into the seething lake.
The cracking sound the sinking ship
Made shuddering above the shriek
Of winds, a sailor later said,
Was like the deadly call of doom.
The cabin and the pilothouse
Were separated from the ship

and spun into the seething waves.
Debris and bodies spread
Across the ferment of the lake,
Imprisoned in the force the waves
Were making as they raged and raged.

A crewman somehow swam and grabbed
The edges of the cabin as it rolled
And spun and pulled himself above
The angry waves and then called out
As others spotted where he was and tried
To reach the place he'd reached, hope flared
Into survival's possibility.

2

The next day, as the sun rose in the sky,
a passing steamer saw debris
and spotted where the cabin was
afloat with passengers and crew
who'd managed to survive the night.
Sheboygan's crew picked up the men
And women clinging to the cabin's frame,
Then started finding others still alive.

A little later Fish Creek fishermen
Cut short their fishing day and took
Survivors off the lake to land.
Eight people lived, eleven died.

The Meaning of Home

1

She'd left her home for Naples, young, a girl
Who'd left the farm and poverty behind.
They'd run away one night, their heads awhirl,
Their dream so stupid it had made them blind.

She'd thought about the fanciful, wild trip
As if it were another kind of lark.
She felt determination in the grip
Of Tony's hand as, starting to embark,

The huge Furnessia churned while engines steamed
Into the ocean's sweeping endlessness.
They huddled in the crowded hold and dreamed
And pushed out of their minds the dreadfulness

Mixed with excitement that was suddenly
Not what they'd felt the night she'd come outside
And ran, the two of them now wondrously
A future husband and his almost bride.

In Glasgow out of Naples, climbing out
Of darkness in the hold into the light,
The gnawing sense of unease, nervous doubt
Departed when they saw an eagle's flight

Above the dock's confusion, winging wild
Into the skies that domed the endless seas
And swept into horizons that beguiled
Dreams stirred afresh to feel an ocean breeze.

But then the ship's crew forced them to the hold
Where those without the funds for cabins jammed
Together: children's crying uncontrolled,
The smells and movements of the tortured damned.

For fifteen days they kept despair at bay.
For fifteen days they waited for those hours
When prayers would be answered and the way
Ahead would beckon like a field of flowers.

But New York's crowded, awful tenements,
Once Ellis Island's nightmare had been passed,
Left dreams and all their childhood sentiments
In ruins; their sense of who they were harassed.

Then Tony got pneumonia as it raged
Inside their building's crowd of families.
They felt their hearts and spirits disengaged
From life, a putrefaction of disease,

And in her heart of hearts she longed for home,
The poverty, the endless days of dread,
A place unlike the cockroach catacomb
That made them both feel comatose and dead.

2

And then the miracle of happenstance.
Her uncle, long forgotten, sent for her.
Her mother, barely literate, askance
At how her daughter's life was like a burr

Into the hopes she'd stored inside her heart
That all the drudgery and poverty
Was not an ending but a place to start,

Asked if her brother might agree to see

If something might be done to save a niece
He'd never met whose circumstance was dire.
He'd not responded as his years of peace
At having left his family became a fire

That gave him sleepless nights and made him hate
Again the day he'd fled into the night,
His father drunk, his siblings all irate
That he had fled and left them to their plight.

Then, on a day so beautiful it shined,
Out in the southern field, old Samuelson,
His Morgan, stumbled, ancient eyes half blind,
And knocked him down, the plowing still undone.

He hadn't meant to write his niece, not then,
But over coffee as he felt his broken hip,
He got up, found his ink and fountain pen,
And recognized the value of his kinship.

3

Uncertainty drummed with the clacking song
The train sang while they traveled ever west.
They saw no eagles as they moved along
The miles that left them feeling tense, depressed.

The endless farms, the woodlands, rivers, hills
Kept flashing past until, at last, they'd rolled
Into Milwaukee with its factories and mills
So new they made New York seem filthy, old.

Years afterward, she'd think about the train,
The steamship that they'd suffered on to sail
When leaving Naples, then the nightmare strain
Of life inside New York, and then the tale

Of how they'd traveled west exhausted, loss,
Their failures clinging to the clothes they wore—
And then the seagulls winging white across
Another steamship's bow, trees on the shore

That towered as the understory teemed
With growth, the burgeoning of energy
That danced small, whitecapped waves that ran and creamed
In crests around the ship upon the inland sea.

Her uncle met them when they reached the dock
In Sturgeon Bay, a taciturn, dark man
That struggled as he slowly tried to walk
Toward the steamer, eyes a strange cyan.

"I never thought I'd see my sister's child,"
He said. He looked at her intensely, turned
Toward a line of wagons, halfway smiled,
And then turned back to her, his look concerned.

"The farm's a long way off," he said. "We'll need
To travel in the dark. You'd better get your stuff."
He didn't speak another word but took the lead
And walked toward the wagons, looking gruff.

Her uncle mostly urged the horses on
While mile passed mile into the forest's dark.
She felt how Tony felt, his health long gone,
The future shadowy, her uncle stark.
He looked lost after they had left the dock,

A man who watched the horses, never glanced
At Tony's still, or her, who didn't talk
But looked as if he were a man entranced.

The farmhouse that they reached before the dawn
Looked small and lonely in the dark and cold.
As Tony tried to help, her uncle saw how wan
He looked and frowned, annoyed, as, grabbing hold

Of horses' reins, he hobbled painfully
Toward the barn to bed them just before
The sun was rising, apprehensively
Aware he'd brought the unknown to his door.

4

In New York's slums the winter cold had cut
Into the flesh and felt as if a skin
Of filth had plastered all the smoky smut
Inside a city filled with deadly sin.

The poverty she'd known in Italy
That once had driven her to flee her home
Became a memory she bitterly
Regretted running from into the gloom

That was the country she'd dreamed, obsessed
About as she and Tony plotted flight
And tried to launch themselves upon a quest
for futures fired by freedom's festive light.

But now the cold was different, sharper, like
A knife that freed the spirit, let her ride
A seismic resonance, a soaring seiche
That let her feel rewarded, sanctified.

At first her uncle seemed to disapprove
Of Tony and his struggles as he tried
To help around the barn or house, to move
A bale of hay or work in fields outside.

But Tony, angry at his weakness, worked
And worked until his former strength returned.
Her uncle saw her husband never shirked
A task or failed to grasp a skill he'd learned,

And slowly, as the days turned into weeks,
The farm and land became a spirit where
A host of creatures, birds, swamps, lakes, and creeks
Eliminated darkness, fear, despair.

She asked her uncle why he'd never wed.
He laughed and told her he'd assumed a wife
Would end up wishing he was gone and dead.
He'd not deliver her "a quality of life."

"Norwegians, Finns, the Germans live nearby,"
He said. "They've got their sensibilities
That don't come close to where my feelings lie
Mixed in with all my liabilities."

One day she fixed their breakfast, sent the men
Out to the barn, then walked up on a hill
That looked out on the lake at her demesne,
Her essence warm inside the morning's chill.

She startled as she looked out at the lake.
That night a sheath of ice had frozen white
The universe and stopped the endless break
Of waves upon the pebbled shore, the light

So dazzling that it caused a dance of suns
Before her eyes, all life transformed, her heart
Aware that this was where her future sons
And daughters would be born and get their start

Toward a future she and Tony once had dreamed
While in a land their kids would never know
But hear of as a tale that had redeemed
Their parents' lives a long, long time ago.

The Coming of Christmas
to Washington Island

The fog was thick when Elinar, still tired,
Came out into the early morning dark.
Einarsson Laine, her father, came around
The Ellis house's corner from the barn,
Both Gar and Coffey ready to be hitched
Into the wagon's traces, two dark shapes.
The wagon bed was fixed on runners sloped
For sliding smoothly on the lake's hard ice.

The air was warmer than it should have been.
When they had come across the lake the cold
Had been so fierce each breath had hurt.
She'd huddled in the Finnish blankets brought
Across the ocean to this wilderness
And concentrated on the bed she'd have
In Ephraim once they'd gotten through the day.

The horses stamped, and then her father smiled.
"Let's go," he said as Mrs. Ellis left
The house's warmth to see them drive away.
Lars Ellis closed the barn doors, walked to where
Her father sat upon the driver's seat.

"Be careful. Fog's as dangerous as cold,"
He said. "You have to watch the ice for cracks.
We'd like to see you stay another day."

Her father looked at Elinar and frowned.
"It's Christmas soon," he said. "The islanders
And Ella need the goods we've got to bring."
He turned and looked at Mrs. Ellis. "Thanks

For all you've done," he said, then flicked the reins.
The horses walked into the thick, dark fog.

As Elinar turned back to wave goodbye,
She saw how Mrs. Ellis waved a cross
Into the air and clutched her hands in prayer.

Her father hugged the shoreline's rocky bluffs
While horses walked on ice that seemed
A lighter shadow of the early morning dark.
The horses plodded on while Elinar
Absorbed the silence of the universe.
Her father was as silent as the earth.
His craggy face with deep set, earth-brown eyes
Stared straight ahead toward the horses' heads.

Her mother had objected when Jon Crist
Had busted up his leg, and she had begged
To join her father on his Christmas trip,
But Jon had come up lame the night before.
The trout and whitefish caught to fund supplies
Were packed in barrels in the wagon's bed.

The trip to Ephraim took an arduous day.
Her father did not want to go alone,
So, after mother-protestations died,
She'd climbed up, layered in a mass of clothes,
Upon the wagon seat and sat encased
In dreams about the Ellises and town.
She thought her mother's fears ridiculous.

At dawn the fog did not let up, but seemed
A little lighter even though they still
Felt caught inside a jar that moved ahead
Of them into an endless murkiness.

Her father looked toward the sky and sighed.

"It ought to lift," he said. "The air's too warm,
But still, it shouldn't be this thick all day."

A little nervous Elinar looked south
Toward where pine and cedar forests stood,
But in the fog, she couldn't see the trees.

"How do you keep from getting lost?" she asked.

"The horses know their home," her father said.
"They'll take us safely even in this murk."
He reached below the wagon seat and brought
The Christmas cookies out and handed one
To Elinar. He kept one for himself.
"We'll be all right," he said, his voice as firm
As muffled horse's hooves on crusted ice.

Time stretched into a tedium that seemed
As endless as the gloominess of fog.
Her father stared ahead to try to see
Some feature that could tell them where they were.
As Elinar kept looking at the fog
She started dreaming of the towns and fields
They'd passed inside the train until they'd rode
Into Wisconsin's forests thronged with trees
So huge they seemed to canopy the sky.
She dreamed of Ellis Island where the Finns
They'd traveled with across the seas dispersed
Into the ceaseless noise of people strained
Through lines that led, they hoped, to paradise—
And then the grimy city with its smoke
And noise and awful smells until they'd found
The great steam engines belching smoke and noise.

Hours passed. Her father asked her, off and on,
If she was still all right. His voice, inside
The muteness of the universe, aroused
Her from her dreams, but then the dreams came back,
And she was in the boat with Uncle Kal,
Her mother, and her father as the sun
Poured light on dancing waves so bright it seemed
As if the rocky island welcomed them
And told them that they'd found, at last, their home.

Her father pulled two pasties from behind
Their seat and handed one to Elinar.
They ate but kept on moving on the ice.

"I've never seen a fog that never ends,"
Her father grumbled. "Even winter sun
Should burn away the denseness in this fog."

What strangeness? Elinar thought to herself.
She wondered if they'd come to Hedgehog Bay[5]
And started crossing to the island's shore.
Her hands and feet stung from the biting cold.

A cracking woke her up, the noise soft, hushed.
The horses stopped. Her father was alert.
He tried to see through fog, his body tense.
Gar snorted. Then another cracking sound.
Her father hurriedly climbed down to ice,
But then the wagon shuddered, creaked, then groaned.

"Get down!" her father roared. "Toward the back!"

---

[5] Hedgehog Bay is today known as Gills Rock.

Heart beating, Elinar slid off her perch.

Her father grabbed her hand. "We'll run, then jump,"
He said, his voice as calm is if they were at home.
They hadn't taken half a dozen steps
Before she saw the crack jagged through the ice.
She didn't think, but jumped, her father's arm
So strong he sent her flying past the crack.
She hit the ice so hard she couldn't breathe,
Her father sliding just behind her slide.
She felt her tears but didn't shout or cry.
Her father struggled to his feet and looked
Toward where Gar and Coffey stood dead still.

"My God," her father said, his breathing hard.

As Elinar got up immenseness swirled
Around her even though the fog was thick
Enough to swathe her in a world so small
It hardly let her see the horses' shapes.
She felt like running, screaming back to land,
To Mrs. Ellis and the safety of her house.

Her father looked at her. "Don't run," he said,
His voice stern. "Breathe. You've got to breathe and think."

She gasped. The horses were alone, she thought.
They'd built a cabin near her uncle, spent
A year improving land and clearing trees,
Her mother careful with the garden seeds
They'd bought before they'd climbed aboard
The train that moved them west, her first crop good
Enough to help them through a thin, mean year.
Her father then had fished for long, long hours
To earn the money they had had to have

For horses, going out in other people's boats
Until the ice had come, then chopping holes
Into the ice to pull the trout and whitefish out.
The horses and the fish were keys to life,
And now the horses stood across a crack
So dangerous the fog was charged with death.

Her father looked away from her toward
The wagon, horses, and the jagged crack.
He didn't speak but stared into the fog.

"We should have moved away from here by now,"
He said at last. "We need to try for land
Or try to work our way around the crack
To see if we can save the horses' lives.
Sometimes you need to think about your life
Before you try to save your animals."
The anguish in his voice was palpable.

Shock stunned through Elinar's morose despair.
"We'll go around," she said. "The horses live."

Her father looked at her. She was beside
Him now, her eyes locked forcefully on him.

He frowned. "Your mother's here," he said and touched
His heart. "She's telling me to save you first."

She didn't speak but started walking south.
"You can't just let the horses die out here,"
She said. He hesitated, caught her by the arm.

"We're miles from land," he said. "The crack surrounds
The horses. You can feel the shiftiness.
That's why the horses stand completely still.

I should have cut the harnesses and let
Them have a chance, but didn't think before
I got us to the safer ice." He paused.
"Out here there is no wood to make a fire."

The resolution Elinar had felt
Seeped out of her into the endless fog.
"Both Gar and Coffey have to live," she said.
She blinked and tried to keep her tears away.
Her father let her arm go, looked toward
The horses one more time, then shook his head.

"The question is," he said. "Where do we turn?
I think we left the headland hours ago.
The island's surely closer than the land,
But if this crack is long enough it might
Cause us to miss the island in the fog."

"I'm going home to mother," Elinar
Said softly. In her mind she saw herself
Inside the cabin pouting as she fought
Against her mother's certainty the trip
To Ephraim was too perilous for her.

Her father stared at her. "Okay," he said.
"We'll follow where the crack leads south." He paused.
"That way we'll be well placed to turn toward
The headland if the crack's too long to cross."

He took her hand and started walking. Gar,
Then Coffey, turned their heads to watch them go.
The fog felt ominous, a presence not
As static as she'd thought, but more alive.
They walked inside a timelessness that stretched
The silence out and made her thoughts a fog.

She thought they might have gone a mile or so
When suddenly her father stopped, then walked
Toward the crack, his movements careful, slow.

"It's gone," he said. "The crack is gone." He looked
At Elinar. "I wonder if. . ." He stopped.
They couldn't see the horses. "What is safe?"
He asked. He reached and took her hand again.
"We've got to try," he said. "It's Christmastime."

They walked east, then turned north toward the place
Where Gar and Coffey waited in the fog.
Her father moved so slowly Elinar
Felt panicked that they wouldn't be in time
To save the horses from the deadly lake—
But then he stopped. A wide, dark opening . . .

Her father backed away. Fog snatched her breath.
They couldn't see the horses through the fog.

Her father looked at her, grief powerful
Inside his eyes. He glanced toward the west.
"We'll try for home," he said. "I don't know how
To save the horses." Numbness, fear, the fog
seemed overwhelming, evil, endless, blank . . .

Time lost its meaning as they moved, the cold
Intensifying as the light decreased.
Her father kept on asking, "Elinar
You're still alright?" and took her hand if, lost
In concentrating on the ground, she kept
On moving but ignored his worried words.
Sometimes she saw the horses' eyes as ice
Gave way and water dragged them to their deaths,
Their thrashing useless in the numbing cold.

"The stars!" Her father stopped. "The fog is gone!"
She tried to understand her father's words
And looked into the sky, the distances
Above her meaningless and fiercely cold.
"We're going right," her father said, his voice
Exuberant. He pointed at the sky.
"The north star's there. We haven't lost our way!"
He turned to Elinar and hugged her tight.
Her blanket didn't really keep her warm,
She thought. She thought about how good she'd feel
If she layed down on ice and went to sleep.
Her father grasped her arm and made her move.

She didn't see the sleds across the lake,
Nor even think about the light of dawn.
She heard her father shout, and then rough hands
Were bundling her beneath large, handmade quilts.
Both Gar and Coffey, with their warm, brown eyes,
Kept looking at her as they sank and drowned.

She woke. She tried to understand the warmth
She felt, but then saw how her mother leaned
Above her, looking down into her eyes.
She started crying as her mother bent
And hugged her like she'd never let her go.

"You're safe," her mother whispered. "Home and safe."

The panic Elinar had felt inside the fog
Swelled up and seemed to fill the cabin's warmth.

"The horses died," she cried. "Out on the ice.
We left them. Then both Gar and Coffey drowned."

"You're here," her mother said. "Your father's here.
We've got to count the blessing that we have."

"This isn't Christmas!" Elinar cried out.
"I should have listened. Stayed at home with you."
She tossed and turned in bed for hours, then dreamed
Of fog and ice and great, brown eyes that stared
At her as frigid waters clutched toward the bed.
Her mother didn't leave her side all day.
Her father, still unsteady on his feet,
Kept looking in on her, and asked each time,
The way he had out on the lake, if she
Would be all right; she never answered him.

Then, from a swirl of muddled dream, she felt
Her mother shaking her awake. She groaned.

"It's Gar and Coffey!" Mother said. "They're here!
Its Christmas day. Your father's with them now.
Outside. They've come across the ice to home."

Her mother's words dispelled the fog she felt.
She looked into her mother's shining eyes.
"They're home?" she asked. "They're really home?"

"They brought the wagon, presents, and the food."

Her heartbeat beating, Elinar got up,
Her mother's arms supporting shaky legs.
Outside, inside the horse's shed, Gar stood
By Coffey, calm as if they hadn't nearly died,
Their heads bent down, her father forking hay.

The fog was gone. She still felt weak, but flames
Inside the fireplace warmed the cabin's rooms.

"It's Christmas," Elinar said happily.

She looked up at the sky. The Christmas star
They'd seen out on the ice was shining, bright
Above the shed where Gar and Coffey stood.

Meeting Walt Whitman in the Wilderness

I ran across the man out in the forest
While hiking south from Ephraim down toward
The stores at Sturgeon Bay, the path ahead
As colorful with red and yellow leaves
As any other stretch of trail I'd seen.

"I have been studying how I may compare,"
A voice declaimed out of a maple tree
So large its branches gnarled into the sky.
"This prison where I live unto the world,
And for because the world is populous
And here is not a creature but myself,
I cannot do it. . ."[6]

        Startled, heartbeat wild,
I looked around to find the man declaiming
The words of Shakespeare in the wilderness.
The voice was deep and felt ferocious.
I looked up, saw a portly man above
me on a branch as wide as any stage.
Red hair, red beard, eyes smoldering with passion,
The man saw that I'd found him in the tree
And with his hand raised up, jumped down and fell
Upon the ground, stood up, brushed off his knees,
And laughed so loud it seemed to make leaves shake.

"Walt Whitman here!" he shouted. "In the flesh!"
"I celebrate myself, and sing myself,
And what I assume you shall assume,

---

6 William Shakespeare, "Richard II," Act 5, Scene 5

For every atom belonging to me as good belongs to you."[7]

The earth seemed tilted as I tried to look
And guarantee my ears were hearing what
I thought they were, my eyes were seeing what
Looked like a man that didn't seem quite real.

The man bowed deep as if before an audience
"That is just the way with some people," he said.
"They get down on a thing when they don't know nothing about it."[8]

"And anyway," the man said. "Widow Douglas
Can't "sivilize" me long as she chews her snuff."[9]

"What?" I began to say, but then the man
Held up his hand, demanded silence, walked
A stutter step toward him on the trail,
Stopped unexpectedly, and held his arms
Up in the air again. He turned around.
There seemed to be a hint of music floating
Out of the maple tree into the air.

"Life's but a walking shadow, a poor player,

That struts and frets his hour upon the stage,

And then is heard no more. It is a tale

Told by an idiot, full of sound and fury,

Signifying nothing."[10]

      Then, as if

He'd never been, there was a puff of smoke,

And with a whoosh the man was gone. Was gone!

---

[7] Walt Whitman, "Song of Myself".
[8] Mark Twain, *The Adventures of Huckleberry Finn.*
[9] Mark Twain, *The Adventures of Huckleberry Finn.*
[10] *William Shakespeare, "Macbeth", Act 5, Scene 5.*

This happened on a day when ghosts were loose
Out on the trail between the villages
Of Ephraim, Sturgeon Bay inside a forest
That towered virgin trees into blue skies.

Encounter with a Gray Morph Owl

He saw the gray morph owl, its yellow eyes
A specter deep in darkness, as he climbed
The ridge where birch trees ghosted, bent as skies
Shrieked cold and lake waves slammed against black stones.

Its whitish face, curved bill, and pointed ears
Leapt out at him the moment that he seized
The steep-slope sapling. Senseless, ancient fears
Gasped through his veins and, beating, spiked his heart.

Inside its cedar trunk, the owl, three times,
Sang, startled at his human face, and spread
Its wings as if it had the strength to climb
Past dread into invisibility.

He wondered at the madness that had forced
Him out into the storm, his restlessness
So powerful it stirred his sleep and coursed
Through legs that moved him out the door.

Ghost feathers touched his face and spooked the song
Wrung from the owl into his blood as whiteness
Whipped wildly out of sight in wind along
The ridge's denseness edged against the sky.

He stood, knee deep in snow, the slope so steep
He hardly had the strength to stay upright
And longed to feel the warmth of lovely sleep
Out of the bitter cold, beneath the snow.

The roaring waves, the wildness of the night,
Knifed down past flesh to marrow in his bones.

He turned and trudged toward the kitchen light
That meant a fire and shelter from the storm.

Back home, beside the fireplace, darkness seared
Into his thoughts. He took his pocketknife
And started whittling the way an owl's eyes sheered
Out wildness from the spirit of a man.

Carver of Birds

He sank into the raven's eyes.
Their surface sheen reflected snow
Back at the whiteness of the skies.
A concave warp of vertigo

Uncovered mice in tunnels cached
From clawing eyes that beaked black wings
Above the scurrying that snatched
Blood past the raven's ravenings.

Inside his heart black feathers stirred
Into his hands, his human life.
A crucible croaked from the bird,
Its blood inside his blood a knife

That tunneled black rimmed raven eyes
Into a cedar block that pulsed with wings
And raucous swells of clawing cries
That made the forest's stillness sing.

He shrugged his spirit from the bird
And left it listening to snow.
He walked through darkness, undeterred
By failing light, the golden glow

Of moonlight through the limbs of trees.
Outside the house he stopped and stared
At birds he'd carved into the eaves.
In rooms, on fence posts, wings were flared.

As birdsong choired cacophony
Into the silence of the night,

The house moved, spirit-fantasy
Of birds eternally in flight.

The Sturgeon Bay Canal

The gash, a wound, had yawned between the bay
and lake for years, the dreamers, politicians, land
a stew of what might be, what was, and how the hand
of humankind could change the earth, essay
a future different than the wonderland
of lake, bay, streams, and endless timberland
that stretched into peninsula, the stay
of land as permanent as night and day.

But then, great metal beasts began to steam
great shovels down into the earth, and sound
began to scream apart the age-old seam
of silence where unbroken land was bound
into a whole until the gash became a stream
where wooden ships sailed through what once was ground.

The Ballad of the Barn

"They've always been half nuts," she said.
He frowned, looked pained, and shook his head.

"No matter what, they're still my brothers,"
He said. "I almost hear my mother's
Exasperation as she thinks
About the neighbor's tongues, the stink
They've put the family in again."

As pretty as an elf, her grin
Lit up her face and dark green eyes.
She looked up at the winter skies.
"Storms come and go," she said, "and tongues
Will wag as long as songs are sung."

"But Willie drove the tractor through
The barn's west wall!" he wailed.

                    "The brew
That Sammy brews could make a knave
Out of a saint inside his grave,"
She laughed. "They had a high old time
Until their words became a crime
Against their sense, and Sammy blocked
The barn door, shotgun ready, cocked. . ."

"The tractor didn't even stall," he said.
"It smashed right through the wall and fled
Into the fields as Sammy laughed
As if he'd taken up witchcraft
And addled who he was and sent
His soul into dark devilment."

"They've lived together all these years,"
She said. "They're old now. Human fears
Stalk dreams and make them long to see
A day when aching bones are free
Of pain, and memories aren't lost
With morning dew or winter frost."

"You give them credit when I'd like
To treat them like two kids and strike
Them with a pliant willow switch.
The tractor's wrecked inside a ditch,
The barn's west wall is half a hole. . ."

She stopped him with her hand, a droll
Look sparking flitting feelings shuttered
Like screens across her face. He muttered,
Alarmed at how she looked at him.
He'd never felt so ill or grim.

"They're old enough. . ."

                    She shook her head.
"They're ninety-eight years old," she said.
"What is a tractor or a barn?
Ten grandkids hence, they'll tell this yarn."

He startled, grinned, chagrinned, and said,
"My mother's neighbors are all dead."

The Composer

He searched a year to find the cedar tree,
Determined that he'd find a lofty lord
That towered dark and gleaming like a sword
Thrust upward with a shaggy filigree
Of branches singing winds into a sea
Of sky where hawks and eagles soared
And wings stitched sky to land, a linking poured
Into the heartbeat of his fantasy.

He dreamed the tree into the song he sang,
Then fingered ancient rosewood cello strings
Into the filigree of cedar wind
That bowed as cries of distant eagles rang
Into the sky and wove tree, song, and wings
Into a music that will never end.

Sitting on a Bench
Waiting for the End of Winter

Time hides in words spoke on the radio,
Inside newspaper columns gray with print.
The young girl, in the winter, watched the flow
Of snow wisps on the lake, her dreams intent
Upon the booming chunks of gleaming ice
That spring would heave on shore, great, white walls, cold
In spite of how the sun thawed sacrifice
From frozen ground and hazed the air with gold.

The young girl took her radio outside
And read the paper sitting on a bench
As winter waited for the moon-stirred tide
To free warm waters from its icy clench.

The young girl waited on her bench for spring
When she and ice and all the world would sing.

Desperation's Providence

After Most American Indians Had Left the Door

A Celtic Droigneach

Crazed, the old man fled frightened from the house, unsettled
By spirit's substance bled by the luminescence
Of energy, jangling jags nettled and re-nettled,
Made garish by the city's flickering fluorescence.

Furious, he'd run to the dock, waters turbulent
On wet rock, his son's stinging words echoing
Inside his head. He shoved his drumming discontent
Into a raging rhythm fed into his paddling.

Piercing into the moonlit island's illumination,
Ancestral roots, rising from memories,
Deracinated, raging blood sparking rumination
Unlocked from a childhood's flood of fantasies

Fulminating feelings long forgotten,
But still a song inside his consciousness.
He heard a singing unlike the jangling begotten
Of tangling time racing through his need to decompress.

Deciding suddenly, spirit wild, ascendant,
The child inside inspired, the old man, elated,
Grabbed his hand-held drum, descendants
Alive inside the meld decision's dream created.

Climbing craggy cliffs where dark pines cling silhouettes
Against moon-silvered sky, spring serenading
Night as fields sigh slender, long-grass pirouettes
Beneath a breeze's arc of shadow-waves cascading,

Carefree, careful, the old man sought an overhang
Where cedars circled a coal-dark pool reflective
Of sky, human spirit whole, a boomerang
Fastening the eye on an earlier-earth perspective.

Palpitating lightning pulsed eeriness.
Above the old man moonlight convulsed, uncanny,
Until the sky-fire's fury began to evanesce
Into circled cedars, dark-pool waters unearthly.

Unmanned, heart hammering, he stared at the intersperse
Of emptiness between stars, his son's voice gravelling
In silence, "Stupid old man, your useless universe
Is cold dead bizarre," he'd said. "Clueless! Repelling!"

Re-singing songs inside his head, immensity
In his breath, he stutter-stepped into a cataract
Of movement, dancing wildly, whirling festivity
Around the pool as he tried to counteract

Cacophony jangling madness mauling senselessness
Into a waning world of troubled turbulence
As stars shining on the pool began to effloresce,
Crazed from his desperate dance, recovering providence.

Ravens and Snow Geese,
A Christmas Miracle

He felt half paralyzed, his legs and arms
inside a spider's sticky web that made
each movement harder than it had to be.
He'd been like this for months, the darkness stained
Into his head so black he wondered why
he couldn't give up, float into the bay
to find oblivion, a place bereft
of loneliness and painful memories.

The day before he'd forced himself to walk
to Baileys Harbor's streets a mile away,
but when he'd seen the lights and decorations,
he'd felt his blackness deepen, cold despair
a rising tide compelling him to turn
from human beings, bare boned trees, and move
to where the freezing skies along the shore
stretched gray above Lake Michigan's dark waves.

He knew he ought to shake away despair
and find a life that he could live again.
He'd lived through decades wrapped in happiness.
Janelle, his wife, had kept him balanced, let
him go to work each day and then come home
to homemade bread, a house that gleamed, and love
so common seeming that there couldn't be
another way that life could ever be.

"We've got it good, Elijah," she would say.
"Two poor kids who've escaped their roots and found
out who they are inside the love they have."

And they had truly had it good, their days
filled with the hours he spent at carving birds
that danced and squawked and flew through every room
inside their house, his wife, the way she moved, a light
that chased away life's shadows, brought alive
the art and craft of living real-life dreams.

But then the moment when reality
had shifted, shattering apart the myth they'd built.
He'd come home from the gallery and felt
into a block of bird's eye maple, thrilled
to find a raven's bright, brown eyes between a streak
of color that was perfect for a raven's beak.
Caught in his carving, time became alive
to what he'd seen out walking in the woods.
The raven spirit in the wood seemed strong
enough to guide his carving tools and hands
into a masterpiece that seemed alive.

He'd finished working on the curvature
that smoothed into the raven's knife-like beak
when, suddenly, he'd heard Janelle cry out,
her voice so soft he'd paused before he'd put
the half-formed raven down and walked toward
the kitchen, following the sound she'd made.

How can life turn upon a moment? Change
so thoroughly that what was sure was gone?

Collapsed upon the kitchen floor, her eyes
had been as lifeless as the wooden eyes
he'd tried to make alive in wooden birds.
He couldn't quite remember what he'd done
when he had seen her lying there so still,
her death a presence in a place where life

and love had been so constant through the years.
He'd heard the siren of the rescue squad
and saw Jim Harmon's beefy face look up
at him and tell him that there was no hope.
He must have called the rescue squad and tried
to see if he could find Janelle inside the eyes
that hadn't closed when she had cried and fell.

He'd spent a year in mourning, living through
parades of friends that came to comfort him—
and then the eerie silence of a house
alive with birds that weren't alive at all.
He couldn't step inside the carving room
where, on the chair he'd been on when he'd heard
Janelle's soft cry, the undone raven sat.
He couldn't stand to think about that day.

At first, he'd told himself that life went on,
that time would heal the devastating hurt,
but lifetime love, despite the promises
young lovers make to spark alive their love,
is rare, and living life once such a love
has ended through the knife twist of a stroke
is more a burden than continuance.

Now, though he'd gotten up at dawn convinced
he'd try to start to climb depression's walls
and find some energy to face the day,
the heaviness he felt was just too much.
The reason for the life he'd lived was gone.
He'd thought that Christmas might be spark enough
To lift his spirit from depression's grip.
Janelle at Christmas once had swirled them both
Into a pageant of activities.
They'd baked and carved and sang at church and worked

to give the poorer Harbor kids
a feeling that the season's joy was true.
But now? He sat upon the bed and stared
at what? The floor? The gray light filtering
through windows that he hadn't cleaned all year?
He groaned. He'd get up, make his coffee, try
to stumble through another dreary day.

Beside the carving room he stopped and looked
at where the raven from that fateful day
stood halfway done, its wooden eyes alive.
He'd not been in the room containing what
reminded him of what had changed his life
and sent it spiraling to emptiness.
He took a step toward a kind of bird
that wasn't all that common in the fields
and woods he'd lived in since he'd come back home
from Viet Nam and left the hated war behind.

Inside the room he froze.

                    "It's Christmastime,"
Janelle's voice said. "Thank God it's Christmas time."

He wasn't nuts, he told himself. The room
was just a room. He couldn't hear Janelle.
Disturbed, he turned back to the hall, then stopped.

"You need to find a raven. Walk outside."

He didn't hesitate, but left the room
so quickly that he stumbled down the stairs.
Heart thumping, frightened by what couldn't be,
he put the coffee on to boil, then got
the toaster out to make a piece of toast.

He thought of how Charles Dickens' Christmas ghosts
had changed a flinty heart into a soul
that celebrated Christmas every day.

Then, calming down, he shrugged. "Okay,"
He said. "A raven then." He drank his coffee, ate
the toast, then got his coat hung by the door.

Outside huge clouds sailed gray above his head,
the wind so sharp it magnified the cold.
He hunkered down into his coat and walked
around the house into the heavy woods
he'd walked for fifty years as snow began
to sting his face with flakes almost like hail.

He wouldn't find a raven. Ravens found
the northwoods sometimes; crows were residents
that cawed and rattled in their flocks through trees
and openings that seldom heard a raven croak.
He couldn't really understand what geas
had led him on the day Janelle had died
to carve a raven's eyes into a block
of bird's eye maple with the wood so rare.

He hadn't walked a mile, though, when he caught
a glimpse of blackness startled through a stand
of young white pine, their branches dressed with snow.

A raven, slender, huge, its shaggy throat
of feathers, slanted down into its beak,
so black they glowed, flared out its wedge-shaped tail
and landed, eyes cocked at the place he stood.
It couldn't be. It really couldn't be.
Another raven flashed out from the woods
and landed by its mate without a sound.

He opened up his mouth. He thought he'd ask
the ravens what they thought they were about.
That made no sense. He'd heard Janelle tell him
to find a raven where a raven seldom lived,
and here were ravens in a blinding storm.

The weirdness seemed to call for some expression.
He hadn't opened up his mouth when wings
exploded just above his head, the sound
so loud it sent the ravens leaping up
into the air, avoiding snow-white geese
whose wings were laboring inside a storm
far north of where they should have ever been.

Amazed, he turned to watch the rising geese,
the raven-wonder driven from his mind.
Snow geese near Christmas like a magic tale!
He stood inside the storm and felt the clouds
move through the sky, dispersing light
into a wonderland of glittering snow.

He turned and walked back to the woods behind
his house, depression lost to swirling thoughts
of all the years of love he'd known and loved.
His memories of years of Christmases
invaded him and made him feel alive.

Inside the house he climbed the stairs
and walked into the carving room and looked
into the raven's face. In every room the birds
he'd carved through scores of years had shed
their woodenness and sang, scratched, winged, moved, blinked
and flew into the stillness that was theirs.

Janelle was silent. Still, Ezekiel heard
her voice inside his head; he felt her love
and sent his love to her at Christmastime.

Note: This poem was inspired by a story told by Robert Blei in "Albert Zahn: The Man Who Carved Birds," in <u>Door Way: The People in the Landscape</u>, Chicago: Ellis Press, 1981.

Planting the Wings of Monarch Butterflies

In Southern Door, an aging man, face fixed,
Pulled up beside a country road and walked
Toward a wooden fence where milkweed mixed
With grass and weeds, fall's fiery colors stalked
Into a forest's weave of summer green,
The season's changing edged into the day.

Beside the fence the man bent down, serene,
Intent on picking milkweed pods, a fey
Gleam in his eyes. He got into his car
And drove until he found an empty field,
Stopped, pulled a pod out of a mason jar,
And freed milk fluff into a wind that wheeled
Time through the winter to a glorious spring
That sprung a summer graced with monarch wings.

Reflections

At Newport Beach
Beneath a Harvest Moon

"The storyteller moon," the old man said.
We sat upon the long-grassed beach and stared
Into a sky now dark, the fiery red
of sunset flung at stars the sky had snared
Into a symphony of silver stained
Into a river of eternal light
Above the song of waves that, lapping, trained,
Like time, into the shores of moon-struck night.

"No, not a storyteller moon." He sighed.
"That comes just as the winter starts to howl.
That's when you tell the stories that are tied
Into a tree frog's peeps or black bear's growl."

Moon-struck, star struck, we heard the lullaby
Of waves absorbing us into the sky.

A Transfiguring of Sky

The rising sun on ice exploded fire
Upon the surface of the lake as light
Burned in the clouds, the bowl of sky a choir
Of gold and reds upon, above the white
Expanse that glinted, danced in flowing swells
And turned the universe into a trance
So stunning winter fishermen felt spells
Ensnaring them into the light's romance.

But even as the sky transfigured how
They felt their lives, the grind imbedded deep
In human hands and minds began to plow
Into the wonder that was theirs, the sweep
Of fire from other people's greed a cloud
So dark it seemed to be a burial shroud.

In Edgewood Orchard Gallery's Orchard

As dip-si-doodled as a particle
Inside the zipping universal whiz,
I stretched into a rusty horse and peered
At cultured woods that felt the guttural,
Mute roaring of a monster's metal fizz
That jawed into a garden's winsome weird.

Then, as an old farm's walls grew images,
And glass shapes whirled with colored curves of light,
I felt creation's fires congeal and mold
Into a spirit drawn from circuses
Born from the striving of an artist's flight
Through zoos of sight, sound, thoughts, the manifold
Of what could be if chaos suddenly
Became a rusty horse whose eyes can see.

Dark Blue Canopy

An Ekphrastic from "Breath of Wind," a painting by Margaret Lockwood

Mist was vertical:
azure tree trunks, evenly spaced, rising
toward unseen, unfelt sky, yellow fire,
branches, and great, round leaves
large as boulders shadowing in murk.

With azure eyes, a man
moved through mist,
hair long and braided wild
into a nest above an elongated face.
He touched each trunk as he moved,
huddled, small and blue,
as if trunks could shield him
from eyes, undefined dangers.

Mist, drifting upward, upward,
silent—tree trunks silent—
the man silent.

Silence's intensity:
a single crystal sound shivered,
moving horizontally
through azure trees.

The man startled, climbing
mist toward the dark blue canopy.

The Garden, The Idea Gallery, Egg Harbor, 8/5/22

An ekphrastic poem in memory of Francha Barnard

I walked into this garden
Not sure I expected to be there,

But the sun was shining summer,
The sky was bright blue,
And monarch butterflies
Pirouetted and danced on a soft breeze.

Only a few flowers graced the garden,
And the orange and black wings of the monarchs
Weren't around the flowers
But circled statues of women
Staring intently out of bronze, pewter, metallic blue, and silver
At the nothingness of everything.

One woman had a bull's horns
And wore a sailor's rope-made dress
So long I couldn't believe legs that long existed.
Another had a tiny face beneath pewter hair
With legs longer than the bull woman's.
Her dress, molten metal, clumped and cascaded
To the ground—the color of dark rust.
Eve, the original woman, stared at bare ground.

I stunned the moment I entered the garden
And strained to hear what I couldn't hear.
Monarchs danced on a silent breeze.

Women stared and made no sound.
Flowers bloomed violet, pink, orange, and white,
Waiting for the dead-still women to speak.

When An Artist Drew an Owl's Portrait

A response after seeing Rebecca Job's painting, "Glow," that was on display at the Egg Harbor Library. This started as an ekphrastic poem but carved its own path during the writing process, metamorphosing into a poem about a pastel, "Barn Owl," I saw Ethel Mortenson Davis draw.

A full moon, bone white as fine china, gleams
through young white pine needles branching into night—
but she isn't aware of the night's moon, or its darkness.
A box of multi-colored pastels, half used down to the nubbings:
and she leans over the hand-crafted dining room table,
big light overhead,
staring at black paper,
eyes where her spirit is.

Inside her stillness you can feel the predator's feralness,
alertness tense with consecrated concentration,

and then, as if her prey is shocked,
fate suspended in time,
her hands blur, her whole body moving,
as lines slash into blackness
and smear color, movement
into an owl plunging claws silently
toward an unseen mouse.

In less than a thousand heartbeats,
as the round moon shines,
the barn owl is frozen into black paper,
wings flared, large eyes swimming
with claws, silence, wings, death,

LIFE.

After a Hans Christian Concert

A zapping xylophonic zipped wind
Out of the audience into the woods
Where owls whooed wilderness in dreams
And woodchucks chucked on wood to blend
Their drumming to the dawning understood
That washed and waved inside wild music's streams.

And in the audience, ecstasy erupted
Like lightning out of spirit's cloistered hood
And danced to measures memed to themes
That thrashed and thundered as sounds disrupted
The sense of life's ought to be and seems.

Remembering Emma Toft at Toft Point[11]

"We only did what should be done," she said, her eyes
Still sparkling even though she'd grown so old
Her hair was white, and when she spoke, she told
Of days long past when sun and summer skies
Still held against the creeping enterprise
Development was spreading as the mold
Of avarice turned wildness into gold
And failed to mourn an orchid as it dies.

My love and I, beneath the massive pines,
Hike through the twilight of a waning day
As Emma Toft's great spirit sweeps with wind
Through massive trees as bobcats, porcupines,
Wildflowers, nesting warblers, monarchs stray
Into a bliss—that shouldn't ever end.

---

[11] Emma Toft was a Door County environmentalist that protected Toft Point, her family's property that now exists as one of the few old growth forests left in Wisconsin, and worked with Jens Jensen, founder of The Clearing Folk School, to preserve what is now The Ridges Sanctuary in Baileys Harbor.

The Lights Inside the Night Sky Disappeared

The northern lights were green and blue and white
And pulsed and waved inside immensity
As if the night was something more than night,
A magic show encapsulating mysteries
No human soul could ever understand.

And then, while standing on a dark, cold beach
As waves rocked gently on the rocky shore,
I saw, within the dancing lights, the shades
Of wild musicians strumming, singing storms
Into the air as Pat MacDonald, Cathy Grier,
And all the makers made a joyful noise.

And then the poets, Murre, Orlock, banged
Their hand drums as the heaven's eerie lights
Intensified horizons found in human hearts.

And then the actors came with banners hurled
Into the spectacle of darkness, light,

And then great crowds of tourists walked down streets
Where artists threw their rainbow winds of paints
Into the sky, and small shopkeepers sold
Their wares and everything was everything

Until, as if time had a keeper, all
The lights inside the night sky disappeared,
And darkness silenced glory that had been
As ancient ghosts and long-lost memories
Scrolled coming times into a future night.

The Shore that No Man Sees

I sit upon the rocky lakeshore, waves
Long, curving lines that sweep and sing their music
Into the rhythms of my thoughts, their cryptic,
Moon-driven spirit a metaphor that graves
Itself into the thought that strikes me, raves
Unchecked into a day so wind-blown, gray,
It makes me wonder why the disarray
I feel inside seems dark, a chasmal cave.

Then, suddenly, I see the waves as souls
That sweep into a shore that no man sees,
And as they chant into the beach, the shoals
Of rocks become a shore of certainties,
An incantation on the shore, their canticle
Eternity, immersion mystical.

On Finding an Historical Novel
in Dusty Archives

I wander through the ancient journals, stacks
Of diaries, sheafs of notes, old letters penned
In other times, and search for long-lost facts
And stories that can take on life and wend
Their way into the book I want to write,
The conjuring of spirit that once thrived
So fiercely time could not restrain its flight
Into a masterpiece that has arrived.

Dreams aren't as dusty as the rows of shelves
Containing nests of other lives long passed.
I touch old papers touched by those whose selves
Breathed love, hate, laughter, spores of thoughts that cast
Their hooks into my searching, transubstantiate
Into the spells I'm trying to create.

A Note on Types of Sonnets, Sestina, and the Celtic *Droigneach* Used In Mythos of the Door

Not all the sonnet types used by poets since the form was introduced by Sr. Thomas Wyatt in the early 1500s are included in this volume, but a large selection of those are included. The Hopkins, or curtal, sonnet form appears only once, in "After a Hans Christian Concert," but the others listed below appear at least two or more times. A description of sonnet types and their rhyme schemes:

Shakespearean (or English) Sonnet

a b a b
c d c d
efef   -Three quatrains
gg   -Heroic couplet at the end.

Miltonian Sonnet

a b b a a b b a   - Octet, as in the Italian Sonnet.
                     - Volta
c d e c d e   - Sestet, as in the Italian Sonnet.
e f f   - 1st tail triplet, with three feet in the first line, whose rhyme repeats the last rhyme from the sestet.
f g g   - 2nd tail triplet, with three feet in the first line, whose rhyme repeats the last rhyme from the triplet.

Spenserian Sonnet

a b a b   - End words of first quatrain in alternating rhyme.

b c b c   - End words of second quatrain in alternating rhyme, with repetition of the last rhyme in the first quatrain.
             - Volta

c d c d   - End words of third quatrain in alternating rhyme, with repetition of the last rhyme in the second quatrain.

e e   - Heroic couplet.

Italian Sonnet

a b b a a b b a   - End words of lines in octet.
                     - Volta

c d e   - First tercet for first three lines in sestet.

c d e   - Seco0nd tercet for last three lines in sestet.
                     Variations of the last six lines include:
                     c d e d c e' or 'c d c d c d'.

French Sonnet

a b b a a b b a   - End words of lines in octet
                     (as in the Italian Sonnet).
                     - Volta

c c   - Rhyming couplet for first two lines in sestet.

d e d e   - Final quatrain concludes the sestet;
                     Variations are possible, such as
                     d c c d or d e e d.

Terza Rima Sonnet

a b a   - End words of lines in interlock in patterns of three lines

b c b
c d c
d e d   -Two variations in last lines: d e d, e or d e d, e e
           as a Heroic couplet.

Hopkins Sonnet

I use a modification of the Hopkins sonnet, which is eleven lines but includes, based upon Celtic poetry practice, alliteration in almost every line. The Hopkins is also known as a curtal sonnet.

a b c
a b c
d b c
d c

Sonnet Sequence: A group of sonnets thematically unified to create a single long work. Often the sonnets in a sequence are not given titles but are numbered instead. In this volume all the sonnets have titles.

Sestina: The first poem in Mythos is a thirty-nine-line sestina, using iambic pentameter but also following a strict pattern of repetition of the initial six end-words of the first stanza until the three-line envoi completes the poem. It is dedicated to the English poets Nick Moore and John Looker who wrote sestinas at the same time I did as the three of us explored different poetry forms.

Celtic Droigneach: I also, participating in a study of Celtic forms with the English poet, Nick Moore and the late American poet, Cynthia Jobin, wrote a *droigneach*, which was among the most challenging tasks I have ever undertaken. *Writer's Digest* outlines the rules for the form:

> Quatrains (the quatrains can be combined to form longer stanzas)
> Each line can be 9 to 13 syllables long (consistent within the poem)
> Line 1 rhymes with line 3, and line 2 rhymes with line 4
> Each couplet has an internal rhyme
> The final word of each line has three syllables
> The final syllable sound should rhyme with the first syllable sound
> Ample alliteration is allowed (encouraged even)[12]

---

[12] Brewer, Robert Lee, "Droigneach: Poetic Forms,: May 17, 2019, accessed at https://www.writersdigest.com/write-better-poetry/droigneach-poetic-forms, 12/24/22.

Books Published by Thomas Davis

Non-Fiction:

Sustaining the Forest, the People, and the Spirit (Albany, NY: State University of New York [SUNY] Press, 2000).

Poetry:

Meditations on the Ceremonies of Beginnings (Durango, Colorado: Tribal College Press, 2020).

An American Spirit, an American Epic (Sturgeon Bay, WI: Four Windows Press, 2019).

The Weirding Storm, A Dragon Epic (United Kingdom: Bennison Books, 2017).

Stories About Life and Art (Appleton, Wisconsin: Kuckuk Publishing Company, 2002). A chapbook of poems by Thomas Davis with photographs of Jim Gehr's sculpture. Accessible at http://www.usonia.com.

Two Poems (Keshena, WI: College of the Menominee Nation Press, 1983). A chapbook.

Novels:

Salt Bear, Four Windows Press, 2011.

On Dragons' Ghostly Hides, Four Windows Press, 2023. Originally published as *Inside the Blowholes*, 2013.

The Alkali Cliffs, Four Windows Press, 2014.

In the Unsettled Homeland of Dreams, All Things That Matter Press, 2019.

Apples for the Wild Stallion, All Things That Matter Press, 2021.

Due to be published in 2023: *Prophecy of the Wolf*, All Things That Matter Press.

Biography

Thomas Davis has previously published a dozen books. He won the Edna Fiction Book Award for his novel, *In the Unsettled Homeland of Dreams*, and the Wisconsin Library Association named his poetry volume, *Meditation on Ceremonies of Beginnings*, poems about the tribal colleges and universities and World Indigenous Higher Education Consortium movements in the United States and worldwide, an Outstanding Achievement in Poetry. In addition to novels and poetry, he has written one non-fiction book, *Sustaining the Forest, the People, and the Spirit*, and two epic poems, *The Weirding Storm* and *An American Spirit*.

In addition to his writing career, Davis has been a long-time educator, working for American Indian tribes in Wisconsin, Northern Michigan, Minnesota, Nebraska, and New Mexico. He started out at the very beginning of the Indian controlled school's movement at the Menominee County Community School and later worked with Dr. Verna Fowler to found College of the Menominee Nation.

After that he mostly spent the rest of his working years as the President or Chief Academic Officer of four additional tribal colleges or universities. He also worked in concert with other tribal college, Māori, Hawaiian, Alaskan, Canadian, and Aborigine educators and Presidents to found the World Indigenous Nations Higher Education Consortium that promotes Indigenous controlled post-secondary schools worldwide.

In 2013 Davis retired as the Provost of Navajo Technical University, which has campuses in New Mexico and Arizona, and moved with his wife, the poet and artist Ethel Mortenson Davis, to Sturgeon Bay, the largest city in Door County. Once there, he started writing the poems in *Mythos of the Door*.